Lord'
Lady

ere

GILDED *in* SIN

Gilded in Sin
Heiress, Book 5

Cover Art by Wicked Smart Designs
Editor Grace Bradley Editing, LLC

ISBN: 978-1-923245-79-2 (trade paperback)

CHAPTER
ONE

Isabella ground her teeth at having to attend yet another Season in town. Her third and her last if she had anything to say on the matter. It wasn't to be borne to have to endure yet another humiliating three months in London pretending she wished to be courted by all the popinjays who tried to court her, dance, and pretend to be someone they were clearly not.

She may of course be a little jaded against the opposite sex, and she could not help feeling so after being disappointed by what was on offer these past years. No gentleman had ever even captured her attention, so how was she to give her heart if she could not be bothered half of the time to even give an inch of regard toward them.

They were all so false.

One in particular this Season to be more so than anyone else.

Lord Hartley Whitmore. How he was the elder brother to her sister's beloved husband Lord Benedict she could not work out. At times, Isabella was certain Lord Whitmore was some off-cut from his family, so different the brothers seemed to be. Benedict was loving, a Christian man who was kind and affectionate and tried to help those who had less than he.

But the brother!

As if on cue to her thoughts of him, Lord Whitmore strutted into the Kenworthy's ball, gathering as much attention as the man could attain and not shying away from the admiring glances most of the women threw his way.

"What a flirt." Isabella pursed her lips into a displeased line, glaring at him. He really was the most infuriating man she'd ever met in her life. That he was back in London only made her final Season all the more grueling.

Having to watch him most nights throw a look, bestow a touch on whatever woman he deemed suitable, before disappearing somewhere into the gardens or house for a suspicious amount of time was almost enough to make her cast up her accounts.

The man had no shame. That he was now sort of related to her family was vexing.

"Lord Cust looks smart this evening," Rosalind said at her side, nodding toward the earl who stood not far from them in conversation with a lady he'd been courting for several weeks now and was certainly not looking in her direction, as well her sister knew.

"He's all but engaged. I think the *ton* will hear of the announcement any day now and it will not be to me."

Isabella tried to keep the disdain, the disappointment from her tone, but even she knew she failed miserably at doing so. There was no use for it. Where her sisters had triumphed, she had failed.

Their marriages—all love matches—were highly praised and what other ladies in their social sphere strived for if at all possible. Alas, she was not one of them. Perhaps she'd been a little too prickly at times. A little too opinionated and judging, but that was only because her sisters had married so well that her standards were high.

She could not go low now.

"Bells, my sweet sister-in-law, how I've missed your scowling visage since I saw it last."

"Whitmore." His name sounded like she was spitting mud, and in truth she was. He was no better than the grime one found on the bottom of their slipper. "I'm not your sister-in-law, and nor do I need you to come over to me and speak. We get along perfectly well when you do not."

He chuckled, a deep gravely sound that irritated her. She closed her eyes and fought for patience. She would not chastise him publicly and shame the family. Even if she wished to every time he dared speak to her.

Which was more often than she wanted.

"We do, do we not? Still, I enjoy our little tête-à-têtes. The balls we both attend just would not be the same without your smiling, happy visage to greet me each night. I do not know what I would do should I not be greeted with such affable love from my dearest sister-in-law."

"Again, I'm not your sister-in-law, you dolt." She met his eyes and saw the laughter in his green gaze. The man, for all his annoyances was, damn it all to hell and back, utterly too handsome for his own good. And he knew it, much to his downfall.

"Should you not be over there," she gestured, "with the widow Lady Leveson? She looks like she's pining for your attention and I'm certain you're just dying to sneak off somewhere in this house and do what you've occupied yourself with these past weeks."

Isabella watched him intently. As much as he tried to school his features to one of innocence she wasn't fooled. Many illicit rendezvous occurred in the closed off rooms at these great events, she wasn't so naïve not to understand.

"You're a lady. You ought not know what I get up to here or anywhere."

"I'm also getting quite long in the tooth and know enough. Not to mention those ladies you've been sneaking off with are only too happy to talk about their interludes with you later and not always as hushed as they should."

"Really?" His smirk was bold enough that she fisted her hand at her side to stop herself from smacking it off.

"You're pleased?" She narrowed her eyes on him. "You ought to be ashamed. At least get a mistress. What if one of the ladies you dally with ended in a compromising position? You'd be done for, and let us not forget you've already left England once due to scandal."

"Which I was innocent of, need I remind you." He moved closer to her and as much as she wished she could shuffle away, a large potted palm stopped her ability. "And since you know so very much about my intimate interludes, let me assure you that I'm always careful. I would never put my family name at risk, Bells."

"It's Lady Isabella to you."

"I do like Bells more. Rolls off my tongue quite well."

She met his eyes, noting all the laughter had faded from his gaze. The hairs on the back of her neck prickled and she quickly looked back toward the dancefloor. Isabella took a deep, calming breath, unsure what Lord Whitmore meant by his words, but having the uncanny belief he meant more than what he was saying.

But then, he liked to tease, to taunt, to be false, so no doubt he was trying to rattle her in a new and untested way than he had before.

"Well, I do not like it and you will call me by my honorifics until I give you leave to do differently, which I should warn you, will probably never occur."

He slapped a hand across his chest and gasped. "You wound me, deeply. I do not know why you're the only lady present in London who does not fall at my feet. Do I not charm you even a little? I try my utmost with you and yet you're stoic and cold, very little give in your hatred of me."

His words took the breath from her lungs, and she gaped. "I do not hate you, my lord, but I also do not think about you." The lie slipped off her tongue and believably so, which she was thankful for. She did think of him, more than she ought, even if it was only in ways to throw mud in his direction or chastise him, nothing else.

He watched her and she fought not to fidget with her hands. "I'm determined to have you as my friend. We're both similar creatures I feel. I'm a lone wolf, and you're a lone kitty cat."

"Kitty cat?"

His grin was infectious, and she fought not to smile at him. "Yes, kitty cat. All claws, until they find someone they love, and then they're all pussies."

Isabella rolled her eyes. "I fear you're drunk and that you think far too much about cats. You ought to slink off and find tonight's conquest. You're wasting your precious time with me, especially when it can be spent more pleasantly elsewhere."

"What makes you think that I'm not getting pleasure from our interlude?"

"This isn't an interlude, it's a conversation, and I'm not so green not to know what you do in the bowels of these grand homes isn't pleasurable. I do read, my lord."

He cleared his throat and adjusted his cravat. "I'm so pleased you said so, I was starting to think that you were far more experienced than a maid ought to be."

Heat bloomed on Isbella's cheeks at the realization of how her words were interpreted. "I'm not experienced at all. I'm merely not so naïve to be clueless as many of the other debutantes are each year."

"I'm glad to hear it. I'd hate for my kitty cat to be on the prowl."

Isabella rolled her eyes and patted Whitmore's chest as she moved to leave. A mistake the moment her palm touched the lapels of his coat and the hardness of his toned body that met her hand. Her mouth dried and she had to swallow to force the words out she wanted to say. "I'll leave the prowling for the wolf. Good evening to you, Whitmore. Do try to not catch the pox."

His hand closed over hers, keeping her from leaving momentarily. "I'll try, just for you, Lady Bells..."

CHAPTER TWO

Hartley wasn't in the mood this evening to find friends to keep him company, nor did he feel particularly enthused to be at the Kenworthy's ball, not after his conversation with Lady Isabella, but he'd stay, do his duty as Marquess Whitmore and try to salvage some of his reputation he lost due to his scandal two years before.

He sipped a glass of red wine, watching society mingle about him, but his attention continuously shifted to Lady Isabella Ravensmere. His nemesis and the only woman whom he could stomach a conversation with, even if it were nothing but barely concealed jibes.

Even so, he enjoyed her company, when she allowed him in it, not that he could say the same for her. She could barely tolerate him, and he could not blame her. Not if she'd been watching as she claimed this evening to be doing. If she knew his every move, his occupations when at such events, it was any wonder she disliked him so and saw him for what he was.

A rake.

Not that he did not enjoy the company of women, and for all her prickly skin, Lady Isabella Ravensmere was one of the most fetching women of his acquaintance. And one he'd only too quickly welcome into his bed. Not that she returned the desire, but there were some weeks left of the Season, so he wouldn't discount her just yet.

"Stop. I know what you're doing. I saw you earlier with Lady Isabella and you need to stop vexing her. She'll retaliate with you one day and then you'll be shamed."

Hartley shrugged at his brother's words, and continued to watch Isabella dance with the Earl of Tyndall. "I like vexing her. She's easily vexed, and she looks quite fetching when she's mad. Taming the shrew."

Benedict glared at him. "Don't call her a shrew. She's not one, and that is unkind."

"True, and I apologize, and I'll leave her alone if that will make you happy. I was merely trying to be her friend, since we're all but related these days."

His brother's gaze moved to where his wife stood talking to the Duchess of Ravensmere, a picture of perfection, as all the Ravensmere daughters were. "I understand Lady Clementine will be making her debut next year now, after coming down with a terrible lung infection this past winter, is that correct?"

"It is indeed. She almost died, from what Angelica said. She's recuperating at the ducal estate in Hampshire but will debut next year."

"I'm glad to hear she's better." He spied Lady Isabella with the earl once again and noted the gentleman's hand was particularly low on her back, almost skimming the top of her bottom.

He clenched his jaw, catching the earl's eye and shaking his head at his familiarity with Isabella. Tyndall threw him a condescending smirk and Hartley's annoyance doubled. "I think you need to have a word with Lord Tyndall. He's being too familiar with Lady Isabella." He gestured to where they were on the dance floor. "Look where his hand is positioned. That is grossly too low and her reputation could be sullied if one of the matrons of the *ton* sees what she's allowing on her person."

"I'm certain Lady Isabella knows by now what is and isn't allowed regarding propriety."

Hartley could feel his brother's inspection of him and refused to meet his eye. "What's your interest in Lady Isabella? Do you wish to court her?"

"Absolutely not." The words came out far more quickly than he'd thought they would. "I merely speak to her because she's Angelica's sister, and nothing more." Which wasn't entirely true. He did enjoy speaking to her, but that was more because he loved watching her every mannerism. She was one of London's most beautiful women, eligible, and rich, and a duke's daughter, everything a man such as himself wants in a wife. But she was also so very prickly, had ensured her past two Seasons had been unsuccessful and he couldn't help but wonder if she had spurned her suitors merely to keep herself unmarried.

Why, however, he could not fathom. Did not all women such as herself wish to be wed, have a household of their own to run, the possibility of children?

Not Lady Isabella Ravensmere from all accounts.

"Do not dally with her. I do not wish to have to answer to Ravensmere and nor do you wish to lose him as your friend. You have very few with all the women you've already bed and put your male counterparts against.

Hartley downed the last of his wine, unable to argue that point with his brother, not when it was true. He had put a lot of his friends offside, and mayhap he ought to curve his enthusiasm of the opposite sex.

He frowned at the idea, knowing that it would certainly not happen. He was enjoying life too much to stop rutting about town, which he was very good at.

"I will not dally with her, but I do enjoy vexing her a great deal and she always rises to the occasion."

His brother sighed, shaking his head. "Lady Isabella needs to marry and you exasperating her will not help her in finding a gentleman she does not despise. God knows, all the others who have asked for her hand have been turned down for the smallest of tribulations. You annoying her further does not help our sex in winning her heart."

"If she marries, can I dally with her then?" The idea hadn't occurred to him before, but now that he thought about the prospect he couldn't see anything but the positives that came with the idea. She would be married, protected by her husband's name and therefore any extramarital affairs she took part in would forever be between her and her lover.

A win-win situation certainly.

"Absolutely not." His brother glared at him, his lips pursing into a displeased line. "Remember yourself, brother. You're a Whitmore, and the name ought to be known with pride and respected by all. If you stooped to such a level you'll never win back your reputation, which need I remind you you're still building after you last scandal."

"That was over the winter and no one in town remembers what happened." Not that he could forget almost compromising himself with Lady Aitken after they were caught in a carriage by her closest friend Lady Ponson, whom he was able to keep quiet by doing a similar service for her that he had for her friend.

It had been no trying task, he enjoyed sex and liked to have it as much and as often as he could. Bringing a woman to climax so she wouldn't gossip about oneself may be a form of pimping himself out, or blackmail depending on how one looked at the situation, but his troubles were sorted and pleasantly so.

"I remember, and you need to behave."

"I will try," he conceded, wanting to change the subject. He looked across the room and caught sight of the earl bending down to speak intimately with Lady Isabella. Whatever the gentleman said brought a flush to Lady Isabella's cheeks and never had she looked prettier.

He rubbed a hand across his chest, disliking the tightness he felt there and hoped he had not imbibed too much cheese with his dinner before heading out.

"I should hope you shall. For all our sakes."

His brother started in the direction of his wife, leaving him alone. Hartley took the opportunity to watch Lady Isabella's mannerisms as she spoke with the earl, and tried to decipher what they were speaking of.

The weather, the state of the roads, or perhaps how much the earl—who was just as bad as he when he was let loose in a brothel—wished to please Lady Isabella. Was he spouting how much he liked her? Admired her and thought her pretty?

Before Hartley knew what he was about, he'd started in their direction. There was nothing wrong in speaking with her again. They were almost family after all, and what better way to be kept safe from rakes than being protected by one.

The Duke of Rolle's hand clasped his shoulder and he halted his steps toward Lady Isabella. "Whitmore, I couldn't help but overhear your earlier conversation with Lady Isabella, forgive me but I have a little proposition you may enjoy."

He turned to face the duke. "Proposition? I'm always up for one of those."

"Well, as to that," the duke continued. "Since you bested me last week for several hundred pounds, what if I wagered that sum, doubled it, should either of us win."

Whitmore studied the duke a moment, liking the sound of him winning a thousand pounds, not merely five hundred. "Continue," he advised.

Rolle's attention moved to where Isabella stood, and Hartley's interest doubled. "Lady Isabella is a woman who knows her own mind. In fact, she doesn't tolerate fools well, nor you from the looks of it, and so I think a wager on which one of us can gain her first kiss, wins."

A kiss. With Lady Isabella. Hartley liked the idea immediately and nodded. "I'd say that I would take that wager and wish you well, although I do believe she's quite enamoured of my charms, as much as she pretends to be otherwise."

The duke laughed, shaking his head. "I think you're quite mad, and incorrect, but she has not been as frosty toward me of late, and so mayhap I can win."

The idea of Isabella kissing the duke made the idea sour a little. "And if she believes us in love with her? That a kiss would equal marriage, what then?"

"I do not think a spinster and certainly not Lady Isabella would kiss any man unless she wished to. I think she will enjoy the interlude and be thankful of it, without expecting anything in return. This being her third Season and all, I imagine she's quite desperate."

Hartley's hackles rose. "She's a duke's daughter, I think you may be underestimating her or what she knows to be right when it comes to society and our conduct within it."

The duke shrugged. "Maybe as we get to know her, in our quest to kiss her sweet lips, which I must say are quite fetching, we shall grow feelings, and marriage will be a possibility, but we shall not know that until we try." The duke paused. "So, what say you?"

Hartley studied Lady Isabella and knew to his core he'd like nothing more than to kiss her wicked and sometimes cutting mouth. Silencing her for one moment. As for the duke kissing her...that would never happen. "I say we're in agreement. A thousand pounds to the man who kisses her first."

The duke nodded, clearly pleased with himself and his wager. "I look forward to my earnings. Good evening to you, Whitmore."

"Rolle."

CHAPTER THREE

The following afternoon, Isabella sat alone in Hyde Park, her maid several feet away leaning against a tree and preoccupied by the book she was reading. Isabella, however, was consumed by another pastime altogether, that of people watching. Or more to the point, watching Lord Whitmore strut along the banks of the Serpentine Lake, Lady Leveson on his arm as they stopped every so often to point out a duckling or swan that happened to swim by.

Like he even cared about the birdlife of the park. How fabricated this man was...

Lady Leveson had debuted the same time as she, but had married, bore a son and became a widow all within one year of the nuptials. Some said she exhibited a grieving widow very well, yet today she seemed far from melancholy.

The picture of them together was all so very pretty, and false if Isabella could judge one's character correctly, and she definitely thought she could judge Lord Whitmore's character to be one of untruths to gain his ultimate goal.

That being to bed the woman at his side.

She sighed and turned the page of the book that sat unread in her lap. She at least had to pretend to be reading in the shade just in case anyone happened to look her way and then proceeded to come speak to her.

But in truth she merely wished to sit in the park, alone in the quiet and enjoy the peace before this evening's event undoubtably would steal her equilibrium.

She looked down at her book but moved her eyes to glance through her lashes toward Lord Whitmore after he belted out a boisterous laugh, the tinkling sound of Lady Leveson's soon followed and she ground her teeth. How sad her ladyship needed to pretend that his lordship was amusing. He was far from being so, in fact, a bore would better match his character if she were to give an opinion of him.

He looked about the park, perhaps searching for others who had noted what a lovely time he was having with his current amour before his gaze stopped on her. Not that he could see her watching him with her head still bent down at her book. Or at least she hoped he could not see her keeping watch, for the rake didn't need to think any more highly of himself, and he certainly didn't need to believe she wished to know his every move.

Which she did not of course, but it was hard not to know where Whitmore was at any one moment, especially when he went to great pains to ensure everyone knew.

"Lady Isabella," Lord Whitmore called, striding over to her, Lady Leveson on his arm.

Isabella looked up and arranged a small smile before moving to stand. She brushed down her dress and clutched the book she was reading at her front. Fought not to glare at her ladyship who was not her friend and had ensured she knew that fact the year they debuted.

Right now her ladyship's smile was barely visible, more like a baring of teeth as if she wished to snap at her for interrupting her time with one of London's most sought-after bachelors.

Well, Lady Leveson could have him. She wasn't interested in him in the least and nor did the lady need to look so displeased. It wasn't as if she had called out to his lordship to engage in conversation.

"Lord Whitmore, Lady Leveson," she said, smiling at them both in the hopes she looked at least pleased to see them, even if she did not wish to be waylaid by them a moment longer than she already had.

A bee flew about them and, using her fan, Isabella swished it away. "A lovely day in the park is it not?" She watched as the bee buzzed near Lady Leveson, who screamed and ducked, Lord Whitmore's startled gaze moving to the widow in alarm.

"Are you well, my lady?" he asked, obviously having not seen the insect.

"There is a bee," Isabella stated matter-of-factly, glancing off behind her to ensure her maid was still present. "Did you not see it?"

"I had not. I was too distracted, you understand."

Isabella scoffed and raised her brow. Distracted by Lady Leveson who no doubt would occupy his time for far longer this afternoon in the solitude of her home. The thought of them alone, engaging in whatever nefarious things his lordship did with women was enough to make her stomach twist in revulsion.

What a cad he was. A rake.

She glared at him before the startled scream of Lady Leveson wrenched her attention from the vexing marquess once again. "It's chasing me. I'm certain of it." Her ladyship moved away from them, swishing her hands around as if the bee was flying about her face. It was not. In fact, Isabella could not see it flying anywhere at present.

"I find if you ignore bees, they tend to leave you alone. Stop flapping your hands everywhere and it will be soon be occupied elsewhere."

"Ouch."

She turned to look at Whitmore and found him clasping his eyebrow. "It's stung me."

"Oh, I must go if the bees are wild here today. I do not react well to stings, and we have the Craigmore ball this evening. I cannot be unwell and miss the event. I hope the sting is not too severe, Lord Whitmore." Without another word, Lady Leveson turned about on her heels, called over her maid and left as if the devil himself was nipping at her feet.

Isabella gaped, before looking back at Whitmore. She felt her eyes widen at the sight of his face. Already his eyelid bulged and she could see the sting above his brow, jutting out like a tiny arrow.

"My lord, bend down a little. The stinger is still in your face." He did as she asked and she reached up, pulling off her glove to use her nail to flick the stinger from his face. At first she wasn't aware of how terribly close she was to his lordship, but now she could feel the soft touch of his breath against her lips.

His eyes met hers and she quickly stepped back, placing a suitable distance between them. "I fear you'll need ice. Perhaps you ought to come back to our home, which is closer than yours. I know we still have some ice in the cellar that could help with the swelling."

"There's swelling?" He reached up and his eyes widened at the feel of his face.

"There is quite a lot of swelling." She didn't want to scare him, but as swollen as he now was, he certainly needed to rest and administer a cold compress to his face.

"I should return home and hope the swelling comes down. I do not wish to burden Ravensmere with this small matter."

"I do not think you ought to be alone. What if it gets worse and you're unable to call for help?"

Even with his swollen face, he managed to smirk at her with mischief. "Are you worried about me, Lady Isabella? Do I sense some concern for my wellbeing?" he teased.

She raised one brow, not willing to give him the satisfaction of an answer, even though she was concerned. "I'm no more worried for you than I would be for anyone in your current situation. Do not read into my care more than you should. It would be a disservice to your ego should you do so."

He chuckled and parts of his face did not shift as they ought with the gesture, leaving him looking far odder than she thought he would so quickly after the sting. "Come, it's getting worse, and I think you need to be monitored." She slipped her arm around his in case he decided to faint, and started back to where her carriage was parked. "I shall have my groom inform your driver to come for you when sent for."

"Whatever you say, Bells."

She threw him a sharp glare, but decided to ignore his use of her name in such a familiar way. Instead, she helped him to her carriage and returned home. Their cook would surely have some remedy to help with bee stings and swelling, which unfortunately Lord Whitmore was suffering.

Quite a lot, if his enlarged nose, which had joined in with his eyebrow said anything about the matter.

CHAPTER FOUR

His eye thumped and he could barely see out of it. A shame for he'd never known Lady Isabella to be so attentive to him before, but he could certainly get used to her mothering.

He breathed deep the smell of her sweet scent, roses if he could discern the aroma as she settled a cold compress to half his face, trying to alleviate the swelling. Thankfully his mouth had not as yet been impacted, and Ravensmere, who had settled him in an upstairs guest room, was in agreement that the doctor wasn't required at this time.

"I think it's coming down a little, but it's still terribly swollen. I'm not sure you'll make it to the Craigmore ball this evening." Lady Isabella's plump lips pursed and he couldn't help but get the impression she did not care that he wasn't going to make the ball this evening. "How disappointed Lady Leveson will be that you may miss seeing her. I'm certain this afternoon's plans had left her a little melancholy, after she recovered from her near miss with the bee that is."

He grinned, unable to help but wonder if Lady Isabella was sounding far too pleased by his canceled plans. "You're not jealous are you, Bells? If you want me to call on you and spend some time alone, I'm more than happy to oblige."

Her eyes widened before they narrowed in annoyance.

He chuckled.

"You're a cad. I'd rather you be with Lady Leveson than here, all swollen and deformed while still trying to flirt as if you're your normal self."

"My normal handsome self?" He waggled his brows and before he could say another word, she lifted the cold compress, flipped it over and slapped it down on his face again.

"Ouch, that almost hurt as much as the sting."

"Good." She stood, but before she could take a step away from him he reached out and clasped her hand, pulling her close to the bed. "For all my teasing, Bells, I do appreciate your care."

Her maid who sat beside the window cleared her throat, still reading the same book she had in the park. Whitmore let go of her hand, but not before lifting it to his lips and kissing her palm.

She wrenched her hand free and shook her head. "You need to behave yourself, my lord. You know I'm not interested in your antics or teasing, so do please save up all your abilities for those who are in want of them."

He shuffled up on the bed and crossed his arms. "I cannot believe my flirtations have no sway with you. You cannot be as cold as marble. There must be a heart in there somewhere."

"You do not want my heart any more than I

wish to give it out, especially to a man who would only break it. You're not the type of gentleman who is loyal to one. You're too busy pleasing far more women than you should."

"I do please very well. Are you not even a little curious as to why I'm so sought after?" He ought not speak to her in such a way. He was teasing and bating her into a conversation she felt she did not entirely understand. Possibly did not even grasp the full meaning of his words. Still, he did not stop.

She sat on the chair at the side of his bed and stared at him, nonplussed. "I do not care to know, but no doubt you'll enlighten me in any case."

"I shouldn't enlighten you, although I think you could use some education." And he'd like to be the man who brought that to her. In his bed. He threw back the bedding and moved to sit at the side, his knees pressing against hers. "I should leave. I think my face is starting to return to normal and I have the Craigmore ball to attend. Must keep the ladies happy after all."

"Should you always keep the ladies happy? Why can you not keep but one happy and be satisfied?"

He met her eyes and drank in the sight of her. She was so very beautiful, one of the handsomest women he'd ever met. No, that wasn't entirely true. She was the most beautiful. A shame she hated him so very much and spoke to him with so much disdain and annoyance that he often wondered why she bothered in the first place.

Still, they were sort of related, through his brother and her sister, so mayhap she felt a little obligated to be kind to him.

"Lady Isabella, may I return to our rooms? I need a moment if possible."

Lady Isabella turned to her maid and nodded. "Of course. I'm finishing up here in any case. I will return soon myself. Just leave the door open, and that will suffice."

Hartley watched the maid leave, and the idea they were alone and unchaperoned spurred a part of him he ought to ignore. "Finally I have you alone and all to myself."

She raised one annoyed brow. "And just what do you think you're going to do now that we are alone? I'm not one of your many admirers, Lord Whitmore. Quite the opposite in fact."

"Maybe I'll convert you. It'll be my greatest triumph yet." The idea of having her as his filled his blood with adrenaline. He'd always known she'd disliked him, not that he could fully comprehend why, maybe it was his teasing. His recklessness in society, his inability to behave that went against her morals. But to know that he'd triumphed against her better judgement, that she succumbed to his charms was an elixir far headier than anything else.

She glanced at his swollen eye and he remembered he was far from looking his best. "Even swollen like a monster I can see your interest in me." He paused, grinning. "Tell me I'm wrong. Tell me that you have not thought of us alone. Of what my kissing you would feel like."

Lady Isabella gasped and pushed against his shoulder. He reached up and held her hand there, refusing to let her go. "Admit it. You've thought of us in that way. I cannot help but wonder all our arguments, our disagreements and opposite positions on things is your way of keeping from falling at my feet like every other woman has." He lifted her hand to his lips, kissing her fingers. "Tell me you haven't thought of my tongue teasing yours. Of our mouths fused, hungry and starved for the other. Tell me that even now, you're not even a little interested in what us being together would be like."

She swallowed, before schooling her features. "Are you well, my lord? I think the bee sting has altered your mind, for I do not wish for you to kiss me, my hand or anywhere else on my person." She wrenched her fingers free and stood, striding for the bell pull and tugging it hard. "I think you're delusional and need to return to your home."

"You rang, my lady?" a footman asked at the door a moment later.

"Yes, send a note to the mews for Lord Whitmore's carriage to be brought around front. He's leaving now."

"Of course, my lady." The footman bowed and was gone no sooner than he arrived.

"I'm fully aware of my faculties, Bells as well you know. Do not pretend that as much as we may dislike each other, we lust for each other too. The two do not have to be exclusive."

She barked out a laugh and he heard the nervous undertones. "I do not lust after you." She shook her head. "You're so arrogant to think that.

Not everyone desires you, my lord. I know this may come as a shock to your overstimulated ego, but it's true."

He stood and strode over to her, standing far too close than he ought. "Prove your words. Kiss me and tell me I'm wrong. That you do not ache as I do when we're near."

She scoffed. "You do not ache for me, you're being absurd."

"Oh I ache, and I've come to the conclusion that I do not like not getting what I want."

"And you want me?"

He did want her and now that he'd been honest about how she made him feel, sexually at least, the idea of chasing any other skirts about town seemed moot. He fisted his hands at his sides to stop himself from reaching for her. "It doesn't have to mean anything, Bells. It can be simply a little bit of fun between enemies. I promise not to fall in love with you, which I'm certain you shall not be doing anytime soon either."

"That you can be sure of," she blurted far too forcefully than Hartly thought warranted. "So we shall have a little fun before the Season ends."

She leaned against him, her hands touching his chest. His heart raced. His body hardened and his skin prickled. Oh yes, she made him throb and all he could think of right at this moment is seeing if he could get her to play his game.

"Not on your life Lord Whitmore," she said, her lips curved in a mocking smile. "Nice try though, but your tricks do not work on me."

He watched her saunter out of the room,

leaving him alone. He took a deep, calming breath and adjusted his cock, before following her out. "It wasn't a trick," he mumbled, put out by her denial of him and the truth of his words.

Perhaps the first he'd ever spoken in his life.

CHAPTER FIVE

Isabella did not sleep a wink that night and nerves fluttered in her stomach the entire day. Lord Whitmore thankfully had not attended the ball last evening after his bee sting, and although she hoped he was well, she was also relieved he did not attend. She wasn't sure she was ready to face him again. Not after what he'd said to her in the guest room at her home the day before.

Kiss him?

The man had no shame...

Not that she'd not woken up in the middle of the night, her skin clammy, her body on fire from the wicked things Lord Whitmore was doing to her in her slumber. She had ached and barely was able to rest after the dream and even now, all these hours later, her body still thrummed from his touch.

The reaction wasn't to be borne. She wasn't fooled by him, nor did she wish to marry a man who had slept with most of London. To imagine holding a conversation with a woman, to become friends with them, only to find out that at one point in time she had been intimate with one's spouse.

She shuddered at the thought.

Not that Whitmore was looking for a bride. He was far too busy rutting about town like a mangy dog, and happily so.

She climbed up on her mount with the help of her groom before they started for the park and Rotten Row. She needed to go for a run, to clear her head, to enjoy some peace and quiet in the cool morning air before the city awoke and her duties to society commenced.

As she rode toward the park, the roads quiet bar for a few coal carts and market sellers making their way to work for the day's trade, she allowed her mind to wander. Particularly towards the Earl of Cust who had danced with her the night before and had made several attempts since the beginning of the Season to seek her out.

He was certainly making an effort, and seemed more genuine than anyone else who had tried and failed to win her heart these past two years. Mayhap this Season she too would find love, although so far she'd not felt anything but mild curiosity and friendship toward the earl, that didn't mean they could not have a future together.

Maybe the connection her sisters spoke highly of regarding their husbands would happen in time, not immediately upon meeting who she eventually married.

Isabella entered Hyde Park and started toward the Row, only noting one other rider farther ahead. "I'll stay within view, Thomas," she called out to her groom, who pulled his mount to the side of the Row to wait for her.

Isabella pushed her horse into a trot and took a deep, calming breath of crisp morning air. Her dark-blue riding gown kept her warm in the frigid conditions and today for the first time since being in London, the hint of the change of season was noticeable.

"Lady Isabella."

Thinking of frigid.

She inwardly sighed and pasted on a smile as she turned toward Lord Whitmore. He sat atop a large bay mare, a good hand higher than her own. She fought not to ogle the man. After touching his chest the day before, her hand still tingled at the memory of it, his hard corded muscles that flexed when she caressed him.

And now, sitting on his horse, posture perfect, a wicked, teasing grin on his lips, she couldn't help but admire how very striking he was.

How very aware of that fact he was...

"Lord Whitmore. I'm surprised to see you up at this hour. Surely you should not have swung those long legs out of whatever bed you graced last evening this early in the morning." Her words were wicked, and far from proper, but then, when had Whitmore ever been any of those things? Surely he would not take offense, and even if he did, she wasn't the least perturbed.

"I swung my legs, for your information, my lady, from my own bed this morning." He leaned toward her, his attention dipping scandalously to her chest before meeting her eyes. "But I must say, I do like you speaking of my bed. It brings to mind a certain unmarried prickly spinster who would look utterly at home within the comfortable sheets, if I may be so bold."

"Oh really," she managed to murmur, hoping he did not mean to reference her, but having a sneaking suspicion he was. She didn't need to think of herself in his bed. Not by his own admission. She did enough of that herself these days.

Silly fool.

"Yes," he sighed. "But she's playing hard to get and I do believe it will take me several weeks to seduce her."

"I should imagine it'll take longer than that." She ought not be so cold or bold, but if he did indeed mean her, and by the laugher in his vibrant green eyes he did, she needed him to know that his courting of her was foppery.

She would never succumb to his charms.

Never.

He chuckled and moved his mount to come alongside hers. She pushed on, wanting to walk, to not be still and next to him. Annoyingly he followed and was soon back at her side. The tap of his whip against her leg startled her and she jumped. "What are you doing?" she asked, rubbing where her skin stung.

"Do not ride off and ignore me. We were having a conversation...about seduction and surrender."

"You were having a conversation about seduction and the lady's ultimate surrender. I was merely trying to survive it without casting up my accounts."

He cleared his throat, and she refused to look in his direction. Did not need to see his handsome face nor allow him to see or consider how much she was enjoying his company, despite herself. Even though she stated the opposite to him, being the object of his flirtatious manner was particularly agreeable.

"Then if you do not wish to talk of the women I'm courting, tell me who you have set your heart on. Surely the third Season is the charm."

She threw him a withering glare. "Thank you for reminding me of my failures, my lord. So gentlemanly of you."

He smirked before looking ahead, once again too pleased with himself. "I cannot help but think you waited for me, Bells. That first Season we met, you cannot tell me that you didn't instantly fall in lust with me."

"I believe I thought you a pompous ass. From when I checked last, that did not equal lust."

"There is a fine line between love and hate. Admit it, as much as I aggravate you, there is a small part of your person who wonders what it would be like if we kissed. I know I have wondered about it a great deal. I cannot help but think we'd get along very well."

The feel of the whip, sliding along her arm sent goosebumps to rise on her skin and she slapped him away. "If you do not stop touching me with that whip, I shall rip it from your hands and whack you with it myself."

"I wish you would."

The deep baritone of his shocking response made her gape. "You have no shame, truly, my lord. Sometimes I wonder if you're a gentleman at all."

"Oh, I'm a gentleman and know how to play pretty with the ladies, but we've never had that kind of relationship. We've always been a little teasing and prickly toward one another, but I know a ripe, juicy apple that's in need of picking when I see one, and I see one now. Right in front of me that I'd enjoy nothing more than to eat."

Isabella swallowed and turned her mount about. "Your time would be better spent in Covert Garden than flirting with me, my lord. I fear your words are wasted."

"Nothing would be wasted on you. I can assure you of that."

She shook her head and, ignoring the rules of the park, pushed her horse into a canter and then galloped back toward her steward. Lord Whitmore was scandalous and acting far too forward. She ought to take him up on his offer, tease him with her wiles and watch him run for the hills when she did so. The man was all talk, all teasing just to rile her up. He would rue the day he teased her if she did take him up on his scandalous offer that had no truth behind it.

Perhaps tonight she would push back, see how far he'd take his teasing before he splintered and backed away. For he would of course. The idea that he meant anything of what he was saying was too preposterous to believe.

CHAPTER
SIX

This evening Isabella ensured she was wearing her most scandalous gown. Not that she was allowed to wear anything too revealing, but the low bodice on her empire gown, the small sleeves that sat just off the shoulder and golden silk made her sun-kissed skin shine and her figure one to be admired.

She wasn't the type of woman who looked for compliments, but she enjoyed the few interested glances that came her way upon entering the Felton ball with Rosalind and Ravensmere.

With a start the Duke of Rolle bowed before her, taking her hand and lifting it to his lips without a word. "Lady Isabella, how striking you look this evening. Will you do me the honor of the next dance?"

She stared at him, unsure why he seemed so determined to dance with her so quickly. She looked about, and not seeing anything that would give her pause, she dipped into a curtsy and acquiesced. "Of course, Your Grace. It would be an honor."

He smiled, and led her out onto the dance floor, and spun her into his arms before proceeding to dance. The strings of a waltz started and others joined and soon they were floating about the floor, his ability making it a most enjoyable event.

"This year you seem to have blossomed into a beautiful flower. Certainly not a wallflower this Season, my lady."

She laughed, and even to her own ears she could hear that her gaiety was forced. "You flatter me, Your Grace, but I've not changed myself this year. Perhaps it is you who has merely broadened your outlook in the society in which we circulate and have for the first time seen more than you happened to before."

"Perhaps you are right, and I'm glad for it. Nothing more charming than a flower in bloom."

"Of course," she agreed, not particularly wishing to continue the conversation, not when it seemed edged with meaning and she wasn't so certain she wanted the Duke of Rolle courting her seriously or considering her as his wife.

While he was nice enough, and handsome too, she did not have that giddy, nervous feeling whenever she was around him. She did not feel anything at all in truth, and that was telling.

They were better off as friends.

You have that giddy, nervous feeling with someone else, however...

She pursed her lips and ignored her thoughts. Lord Whitmore was not a man she would consider marrying. He was a teasing rogue who would play with his food and then discard it, and before he could make a meal out of her she would play with him instead and see how he liked it.

"My estate in Surrey has a very colourful and established garden. My mother spent many years getting it to perfection. I would like to show it to you one day."

Isabella cleared her throat and, looking over His Grace's shoulder, spied Lord Whitmore, standing alone with a glass of wine in his hand, watching her. His intense dark stare unnerved her. His unruly locks looked disheveled, as if he'd just rolled out of bed. Which, knowing the marquess was probably not out of the scope of his situation this evening.

"Should you hold a house party and invite me and my family, I'm certain we would more than welcome a visit to your home county. I do not believe I've ever been."

"It is one of the most beautiful locations in England. I should love to have your approval of it."

She smiled but refused to agree. She didn't want him believing she'd set her cap on him and she wasn't the type of woman to lead any man on. Not intentionally.

Are you not going to do exactly that with Lord Whitmore?

Isabella threw herself into the dance. Her teasing of Whitmore was to prove a point and teach him a lesson in mocking the opposite sex, or her in particular, which he seemed determined to accomplish.

She would not be made a fool of, not by him or anyone and it was high time she called him out on his unfitting comportment and see just how far he would go before he stopped pretending to like her and scuttle off to whatever fox hole he clawed out of.

Only then would she start to consider whom she ought to marry, if anyone at all. The duke was nice and eligible, but she wanted to love her husband, whomever that ended up being. She wanted to be in lust with her husband, and unfortunately the duke did not tick either of those boxes.

Perhaps the Earl of Cust would grow on her some more...

The dance came to an end and before they had stepped from the ballroom floor, Lord Whitmore was before them, eyeing the duke with an odd warning in his green eyes. "Rolle," he said, his voice devoid of warmth and unlike the teasing tone he usually always spoke with when around her.

"Whitmore," the duke replied in kind, both men making the room far chillier than it was. "Taking a turn about the room were you? Any prospects this evening who have caught your eye?"

The duke's words were not what Isabella expected, and she glanced between the two men, wondering why they seemed at odds with each other. Were they not friends? She'd certainly seen them at other social events talking amiably. Whatever was their difficulty this evening?

"Just one," Whitmore murmured, meeting Isabella's eyes.

She swallowed the nerves that fluttered in her stomach at his words. Was he openly flirting with her now too, in front of their peers? The man had no shame, and nor would she allow him to get the better of her.

"Then we are in agreement," the duke responded in turn, looking at her also, a small knowing smile on his lips.

Isabella had heard enough and, dipping into a curtsy, prepared to flee. She needed a moment to regroup, to rethink her plan and ignore whatever this reaction was that was churning within her body. A feeling that only the blasted, rakish rogue Whitmore fashioned.

"If you'll excuse me, Your Grace, my lord, I see my sister is gesturing for me to return to her side. I bid you both a good evening."

"The evening is young, my lady and we shall meet again," Whitmore stated, his gaze pinning her to the spot.

She did not respond, and instead, fled like the devil himself was nipping at her silk slippers. If she were to teach Whitmore a lesson she really needed to learn to gain better control of her wits and not let him disable her so.

The duke she could handle, not having those odd sensations when around him made his words almost of no consequence, even if she knew he was clearly courting her. But the marquess was a different matter altogether.

She came to Rosalind's side and moved into a conversation her sister was having with several of her friends. The time away from both her gentleman admirers, which she would refer to them as from now on—even if she believed Whitmore was doing so merely to cause her confusion and grief—helped her regain her composure.

The conversation regarding the upcoming Leveson ball was all anyone wished to discuss. The mention that her ladyship, the young widow whom

Isabella had seen Whitmore with at the park, seemed to be the topic of the night.

Isabella didn't particularly wish to hear any more on Lady Leveson, not after her interaction with her only yesterday. Still, to know she was hosting an event would give her the opportunity to attend and see Whitmore fawn all over his love interest. His real one at least. How could he pretend to court her when his true lover was under the same roof? He would not and it would prove her point that he was a menace, and needed to apologize for being a cad toward her this Season.

Her eyes widened at the unexpected touch of someone's hand at the hollow of her back. She stilled as warm breath swept across her ear. "Are you running away from me, Bells? I must say I'm most disappointed to know that you're scared of me."

She took a calming breath, ready to flame him alive, but instead turned on her heel and looked up at his lordship. She schooled her features, hoped he did not notice that taking in his handsome face was likely to spellbind anyone.

Damn the man and his handsomeness.

"I think it is you who ought to be scared, my lord," she replied. He just didn't know it yet...

CHAPTER SEVEN

Without thinking of what his gesture looked like, Hartley picked up Isabella's hand and led her onto the dance floor. She did not argue—a welcome reprieve from her usually prickly self—before he pulled her into his arms for a waltz.

He was playing with fire and in more than one way. The bet he'd agreed to with the Duke of Rolle was feeling more and more uncomfortable on his conscience the longer the bet progressed. That Isabella was his brother's sister-in-law, a woman Benedict would not wish him to offend, also made guilt prickle along his spine.

But Lady Isabella was also a woman who had long intrigued him, and he wanted to see if she was truly as cold and dismissive as people believed her to be. Or was she merely jaded with society, especially considering this was her third Season.

What he was doing was wrong, and he ought not be faux-courting her to win her first kiss. But in turn, he was loath to lose any wager, no matter what that wager entailed.

He pulled Isabella into his arms, closer than he should and drank deep the scent that drifted from her, roses and all sweetness that he basked in. Should he be truly looking for a wife, a woman such as Isabella, a fiery, independent, strong-willed and intelligent woman was just the type he could tolerate.

If he were looking for a wife.

The bet is harsh. You should stop this nonsense now before it's taken too far...

Her hand drifted to his nape and the feel of her fingers playing with his hair stole the breath from his lungs. He swallowed, fought to keep his heart from jumping out of his chest at the too-familiar touch.

"I suppose this means that we're to dance together, my lord. However, I do not quite remember you asking me."

He couldn't quite remember his name right at this moment, nevertheless a quick-witted response to her statement. Still, he rallied and grinned down at her as if nothing were untoward. As if his body didn't tremble at the feel of her fingers on his neck. As if his body were not aflame with need after her touch.

"Do you not?" He feigned ignorance. "I'm certain that I asked. Perhaps my handsomeness has rendered you deaf to my words and you're merely content to bask in my handsome presence."

She grinned up at him, and he had the overwhelming urge to hold her closer, to keep her.

For himself...

"Perhaps it has."

He raised his brows, having not expected her to

be flirtatious back to him, or at least to keep being so. Surely at any moment she would switch her tactics and be curt, cut him dead with one of her responses he couldn't help but admire.

"Do you mean to tell me that you're in agreement? Well," he chuckled, pulling her close during a turn of the dance, "I'm delighted to hear so."

"And you've been seeking me out so much lately, may I presume that we've laid down our swords and become friends?"

Friends? He could be friends with Lady Isabella, and maybe upon first meeting her he had thought they would be. But after the ruinous scandal he was part of and hightailing it abroad to try to save his family name, he'd thought she would long be married when he returned.

Married and settled and friendship untenable. To find her not so, to find her as prickly as she had always been toward him, possibly his fault due to his belief everyone he met would be charmed by him, had ensured he'd fallen back into riling her up as much as he ever had.

But after his bet with Rolle, and spending more time with Lady Isabella, he knew without a doubt he could be friends with this woman if she allowed them.

Not that the friendship would last long. Not if she ever found out about the wager he was a part of that involved her.

His gaze dipped to her lips and his mind jumped to thoughts of kissing her plump, ripe mouth. Surely she had never kissed a man. Were her lips as sweet and untouched like the rest of her?

"Were we not always friends, Bells? Friends

who are candid with one another, but friends none the less." He slipped his hand farther about her back and edged her close. His body hardened at the feel of her in his arms, the press of her breasts against his chest. For a moment his concentration and train of thought vanished and his steps faltered.

She scoffed. "We've never been friends, as you well know. But I'd like to change that. I believe we're very similar of nature, my lord. You're not as stupid as I once thought you and so I think we can get along amicably well. In fact, being about you may sway other gentlemen to see me differently this year. I may end up betrothed after all."

Hartley cleared his throat. The mention of her marrying another sent a chill down his spine. What if she married someone unworthy? Someone cruel? "The Season is young and if you promise yourself to anyone it'll make our newly formed armistice so much harder to continue. Unless you're open to seeing me in secret after you wed..."

His words were outrageous, but then, when wasn't he so? From the amused grin Lady Isabella offered up at him, he knew she was well aware of that fact.

"You would cuckhold your friend."

The mention of sex, of having her after she'd agreed to be another's sent heat to course though his blood. Hell yes he would cuckhold anyone if it meant he could have her in his bed without having to marry. To gain a first kiss through a bet was one thing, but marriage was not what he wished for. Not quite yet...

She would be all fire and ice too, he had little

doubt. A minx in bed he could never get enough of. He could have everything he wanted without having to give up his life as he now lived it. A boon for any eligible, rich bachelor.

"To have you in my bed. Yes I would."

A light blush bussed her cheeks, but she did not bolt. In fact, her fingers slipped through the hair at the nape of his neck once more, sending shivers down his spine and heat to settle between his legs. "Is it a big bed?" she asked.

He gaped and then remembered to shut his mouth. "Very big."

The music came to an end, and he swept her to a stop. "That's good to know. I do not think I'd like a small one. Very unsatisfying."

He could not speak to form a reply and without another word, she dipped into a curtsy and walked away, leaving him looking after her from the dance floor. Another couple bumped into him, and he remembered to move as the other dancers took to the floor for a minuet.

His body was aflame. His mind boggled. And maybe, just maybe, he may have found his match in more ways than he was willing to admit to himself...

CHAPTER
EIGHT

Later that evening, Isabella sat in the supper room with her sister Rosalind and Ravensmere, discussing the night's events and how wonderful the ball had been so far.

The scent of roasted meats and sweet puddings lingered in the air, though Isabella picked at her crab cakes, not overly hungry. Her mind was a whirl of thoughts.

Around them, the hum of conversation mingled with the clink of silverware on china, the rustle of silk gowns, and the occasional burst of laughter from a nearby table. Candlelight flickered across polished mirrors, catching the gleam of jewels and the gloved hands of ladies lifting glasses of wine.

After her dance with Whitmore, she could not forget her scandalous words... *His* wicked words for that matter. She wasn't sure what she should do or how to behave when around him, but she was determined to see if his courting was merely for his own amusement.

She was certain his flirtations would go nowhere. He was merely playing with her like a cat played with a mouse before it devoured the poor creature. Whitmore was no different. He was a wolf masquerading in lamb's wool.

As much as he might pretend they were friends, she couldn't help but get the feeling he was trying to see if she would fall for his charms if only to gloat about it later. Considering she had been one of the few who had not—and there weren't many—she could see why that might injure his ego.

Could he be courting you in truth?

She shook the thought aside, lifting her glass of wine and taking a substantial sip. The rich, full-bodied flavor coated her tongue, warming her throat. No, an impossible possibility. He did not want to get married any more than she wished to endure another Season.

So what was he doing?

She caught sight of him outside the supper room doors, talking with the Duke of Rolle. The sight of the two together raised the hackles on her back, for the men, earlier in the evening, had seemed less than pleased to see each other—particularly regarding her. Why were they speaking now?

The duke glanced about and caught sight of her watching. He excused himself quickly, melting into the throng of guests who had not yet come in to take refreshment. The marquess, however, lingered. He nodded in her direction, a small mischievous smile curving his lips before he too strolled away, though in the opposite direction.

"Isabella, is something the matter?" Rosalind asked.

She shook her head and took another sip of her wine. "No, particularly, but I do have the oddest feeling that the Marquess of Whitmore is trying to best me in some way."

"Best you?" Ravensmere asked, setting down his fork and giving Isabella his full attention. "What do you mean?"

"I wish I knew," she replied. "But do not worry. I'm certain another distraction will come alone soon enough, and he'll be nowhere to be seen."

Rosalind turned in her chair to face Isabella. "Whitmore is Benedict's brother. Surely he would not make sport of you in society."

Isabella shrugged. "Dear sister, I know you see the best in people, but Whitmore is a scoundrel and one I barely tolerate. He has been particularly attentive to me, and I cannot help but think it's disingenuous."

"Do you wish me to look into the situation?" Ravensmere asked, casting a searching glance about the room for Whitmore, as if he could somehow pry the truth from him merely by sighting his lordship.

Isabella shook her head. "No, I do not think that's necessary. Lord Whitmore has not done anything untoward. He has merely danced and been attentive. I just think it is odd, that is all."

But why now? She had been in society for three years...

"You have matured, and you are a very beautiful woman," Rosalind said gently.

Isabella picked up her fork, not wishing to discuss handsome features as a means of catching a husband. The laughter from the nearby tables grated on her ears, a cruel reminder of how easily others spoke of courtships and matches as if they were as simple as choosing a dish from the supper table. Surely one might find a partner with something more meaningful than mere appearance. Such a shallow way of judging a spouse.

"I do not wish to be married merely because I have a pretty face."

Rosalind smiled, reaching across the table to clasp her hand. "I did not mean it that way, my dear. But you are much more engaged, more confident than your first Season when you were timid and a little aloof. I think any gentleman would notice the change, and see the virtues in it, and perhaps wish those very virtues in a wife."

"Whitmore is not looking for a wife," she blurted before she could stop herself.

"Whitmore does not know half the things he wishes," Ravensmere said, leaning back in his chair and wiping his mouth with his napkin.

That was true. Whitmore was a little flippant of nature. But oh, he was handsome. Even in the crowded supper room, she could still recall the faint scent of sandalwood clinging to him, and the way the candlelight had caught in his hair when they danced. Even if she did not wish it, she could not help but admit she thought of him more than she should.

Maybe she was being too severe on the opposite sex. Maybe Whitmore was vying for her hand, and she was so accustomed to being overlooked that now, when he did not ignore her, she could not help but feel unsettled.

Either way, she would see how long Whitmore continued with this farce. If she were proven right, and she was merely a whim, he would scuttle away like all the others before him. If not—well, if he truly pursued marriage, she would face that troublesome situation when it presented itself. Not that she thought such an outcome would happen.

Not with Whitmore at least.

CHAPTER NINE

Whitmore made it to his club after leaving the ball. He did not feel inclined to attend any further events that evening. He'd had his fill of the *ton*, and after spending a considerable amount of time with Lady Isabella, his desire to pretend interest in anyone else had waned.

Instead, he and a group of his friends—young lords all—headed off to Madame Cheri's for a little evening entertainment on the demi-monde side of society. The gas lamps along the street flickered in the damp night air, the cobbles glistening faintly from a recent shower. The rhythmic clatter of hooves echoed off the narrow buildings, and the faint scent of smoke lingered on the breeze.

The carriage rolled to a halt outside Madame Cheri's establishment. Several gentlemen lounged outside, smoking cheroots, the smoke curling up and disappearing into the night. Ladies hung off their arms, painted smiles hiding sharp eyes, ready to trade their wiles for coin. The sultry laughter of women and the occasional pop of champagne corks drifted from the house.

Whitmore made his way up the stone stairs, his footsteps uneven. He was a little foxed—he had imbibed too much this evening, possibly because his reaction to Lady Isabella, and her flirtatious charms, had been difficult to endure. The memory of her laughter, low and teasing, clung to him like a curse. He could still see the faint blush on her cheeks, the delicate rise of her shoulders when she turned her head just so. Her full breasts, and pretty mouth.

Damn he wanted to devour every little bit of her...

Lord Shaw clapped him on the shoulder, his smile almost stretching from ear to ear. "Come, man, the ladies wait. Do not dally in the doorway."

Whitmore nodded and followed him inside. As was expected at a house of ill repute, the selection of ladies to keep one's company was plentiful. They were all beautiful—silk-clad curves, powdered skin, eyes like polished gems in the dim candlelight—and they were clever in the bedroom.

But as he looked around, seeking one who tempted him more than another, he found none who did. The room was thick with perfume and heat, the air humming with laughter and whispered promises, yet none of it tempted him.

Instead, he headed for the bar, sat on a stool, and ordered a pint of beer. Perhaps if he drank more, and did not rush his choice, the evening could yet end well.

He did not know how long he sat there before Madame Cheri herself slid up beside him, her arm snaking around his neck, her breasts pressing boldly against his person. Her scent was overpowering—violets and amber, the same perfume she had worn the last time he had come here months ago.

"Whitmore, it is so good to see you again. We have missed you," she purred. Her sultry voice was well trained to seduce the hardest heart.

But this evening, her seductive voice and delectable body did nothing to tempt him.

"I am here merely to observe." He reached for his beer while trying to untangle himself from Cheri's grasp.

She chuckled, a tinkling laugh that drew the attention of nearby patrons, but it did nothing to stir his interest. He studied her as she leaned close, the candlelight glinting off the rhinestones at her bodice. Her painted lips formed a perfect smile, yet it was lifeless to him—just another mask in a room full of guises.

He frowned at his own lack of interest. It was not like him to reject what was so easily given. For years he had enjoyed uncomplicated relations under this roof—no expectations, no emotions, just the trade of pleasure for coin and company. But now, the thought of taking Cheri, or any woman upstairs, was something he could not stomach.

He ran a hand through his hair, frustration knotting in his chest. Was there something wrong with him? How could he not want to bed these beauties—to lose himself in pleasure, to be pleasured?

He tried to imagine Cheri on her knees before him, flicking open his falls, but when he glanced down, all he saw were the sweet, perfect features of Lady Isabella Ravensmere.

Her face rose in his mind unbidden—the tilt of her chin, the stubborn curve of her lips, the mischief in her eyes. He remembered the scent of her—roses and something subtler, something purely her. He could almost feel the warmth of her hand as she'd rested it lightly upon his sleeve, the tremor of restrained curiosity in her touch.

He swallowed hard and downed a good portion of his beer. "Not this evening," he muttered, reaching into his coat pocket and pulling out a gold coin. "For your troubles."

He pressed it into her palm. With an impish grin, she blew him a kiss and slinked off to her next conquest, her skirts whispering over the floorboards.

He watched her go, an air of disinterest settling over him. The laughter, the music, the seductive whispers—all seemed to fade into a dull hum. His surroundings blurred at the edges, leaving only the taste of beer and the faint ache behind his eyes.

He should have returned home after visiting his club. But as was custom with his friends, they often ended their nights here after an evening's entertainments.

Tonight was different, though. He was different. Something had shifted. The easy satisfaction of vice no longer offered comfort, and the thrill of pursuit had soured into disquiet. Lady Isabella's face haunted him like a prayer left unanswered.

He finished his beer, slipped a coin across the bar, and stood, starting for the front door. His friends were long gone, possibly already enjoying their night of revelry with the women upstairs.

But not him. Not this eve.

All he wished for was the quiet of his library, a good dram of whiskey, and his thoughts—thoughts that, somehow, in the course of only a few days, were now fixated on a woman he had bet his friend he could seduce. A wager meant as idle amusement now burned with something dangerously close to regret.

As he stepped outside, the cold night air struck his face. The fog had thickened, the streetlamps casting halos through the mist. A carriage rattled by, its wheels splashing through a puddle.

He adjusted his coat collar and walked toward his waiting carriage. The smell of damp stone and smoke clung to him, mixing with the faintest trace of rose he imagined still lingered on his sleeve from the ball.

His driver tipped his hat. "Home, my lord?"

"Yes," Whitmore said quietly, climbing inside. The door shut behind him with a heavy thud.

As the carriage jolted forward, he leaned back against the seat and stared out at the blur of lamplight and darkness beyond the glass. London at night was both alive and dead—a city that glittered with sin and whispered secrets through its fog. It suited him once. But tonight, he felt the emptiness of it keenly, as if he too were one of its ghosts.

He drew in a slow breath and exhaled. "What the devil are you doing, Whitmore," he muttered to himself.

Lady Isabella's voice seemed to answer him in memory—bright, teasing, clever. He could almost hear her laughter at the ball, the way her words had challenged him, the spark that had lit in her eyes when she dared to meet his gaze without fear. It stirred something inside him that was not lust but longing. Dangerous, foolish longing.

He rubbed his temple and looked down at his hands, flexing his fingers as though to shake off the image of her.

The carriage wheels struck a rut, jostling him from his thoughts. Outside, the streetlamps thinned as they left the bustle of Covert Garden behind. The night deepened—quiet, save for the rhythmic creak of harness and the steady clop of hooves.

By the time he reached his townhouse, the fog had rolled thick across Berkley Square. Whitmore descended the steps, nodded to his butler, and made straight for the library.

The fire was still burning low in the grate, casting an amber glow across the shelves. The faint scent of leather and oak filled the room. He loosened his cravat, poured himself a generous measure of whiskey, and sat heavily in his favorite chair. The glass was cool in his hand. The whiskey burned on his tongue.

He stared into the flames. Lady Isabella's smile lingered in his mind, bright as candlelight and just as dangerous. He had wanted to toy with her—to make her fall, to win the substantial blunt. Yet now he could not stop thinking of her.

He closed his eyes and leaned back, the crackle of the fire filling the silence.

"Damn it, Isabella," he murmured, more to

himself than the room. “Whatever am I going to do with you...”

CHAPTER TEN

The following evening, at the Groose ball, Isabella hoped to see the Duke of Rolle.

If he was truly interested in her, as his attentions had suggested, then surely if she were to hint at the possibility of a kiss—a stolen moment alone—he would be more than willing.

She entered the ballroom invigorated by her decision, her pulse quickened by a strange mixture of curiosity and resolve. The gleam of crystal chandeliers shimmered across gilded mirrors, scattering light over silk gowns and jeweled hair. The scent of beeswax, perfume, and champagne hung thick in the air. Laughter rippled through the vast space as the orchestra struck up a lively country dance.

She looked about the room, scanning the sea of feathers and polished boots, but could not see the duke. Nor, for that matter, could she see Lord Whitmore in attendance.

For the next several hours she danced with Lord Cust, and later with her brother-in-law, Ravensmere. The evening passed pleasantly enough—the music lively, her steps measured, her smile carefully practiced—but she was unable to gauge whether the duke's supposed affection was genuine.

Then, after supper, she spied her quarry. Finally, his grace had arrived.

He stood at the far end of the ballroom speaking with Lord Whiteley and his newly minted wife, Margaret. Isabella paused where she stood, her fan motionless in her hand, and watched him. He looked every inch the perfect gentleman. Tall, composed, his dark hair gleaming beneath the candlelight, his expression politely unreadable.

She lingered for several minutes, building up her courage to do what she must. When the dancing recommenced, he started toward her, a small smile touching his handsome face before he dipped into a bow.

"Lady Isabella. A pleasure to see you this evening. Would you care to dance?"

She took his arm without answering, though instead of turning toward the dance floor, she led him toward the terrace instead. "A dance would be nice," she said lightly, "but I have been quite busy this evening until your arrival. Perhaps we could take some air outside. There are many others out there—it would not be frowned upon."

He looked toward the terrace and then back at her. "Of course," he said, clearing his throat. "If that is what you wish."

"It is," she replied, smiling up at him. Her heart beat fast as she noted the faint tension in his jaw, the way his hand flexed against his side as though uncertain whether he ought to have acquiesced.

They exited through the terrace doors, left open for guests to wander in and out through the night.

A soft breeze swept through, carrying the mingled scents of roses and damp stone. Candlelight spilled from the ballroom behind them, flickering over the flagstones beneath their feet. The terrace was alive with people—some taking the air, others smoking cheroots, laughter and low conversation floating through the air.

They walked together, the duke oddly quiet. Isabella glanced up and saw that he looked lost in contemplation. "Is everything well, Your Grace?" she asked.

He turned as if startled, as though he had forgotten she was beside him. "Of course," he said quickly. "I am merely enjoying our stroll."

She did not respond, merely looked ahead and wondered if that was true. He seemed distracted—his gaze fixed on the gardens beyond, his expression distant, as though his mind were elsewhere entirely.

Perhaps he was as nervous as she? Maybe he wished to kiss her and did not know how to go about gaining such a favor?

"The night is warm, is it not?" she ventured.

He nodded, his tone polite. "Lovely evening to take the air."

They came to stand beside the balustrade, looking out over the gardens below. The hedgerows formed dark silhouettes under the moonlight, the soft rustle of leaves and distant trickle of a fountain breaking the silence.

She turned, leaning her hip against the wall. Her palms felt damp against the silk of her gown as she rallied herself to be brave. She had never kissed a man before and wasn't entirely sure how to go about gaining her first. Yet she had resolved to try.

He looked down at her, and as if sensing she might be offering more than polite company, promptly shuffled farther away.

"Have you been enjoying the evening?" he asked, his voice a touch too formal for her liking.

"I have. Though I must say, I was surprised you arrived so late."

"Yes. Lord and Lady Seymour hosted their own entertainment earlier, a dinner, and I was committed to attend before coming here."

"My sister, the duchess, is good friends with Lady Whiteley, and had promised that we would remain here the entire evening," Isabella said, forcing a small smile. "Otherwise, we might have attended also. Lady Seymour is a lovely lady and a most accomplished hostess."

"Indeed she is," he murmured.

Isabella bit the inside of her cheek, glancing away. Conversation with the duke was proving more difficult than she had anticipated. Every word between them felt measured, stiff, as if they danced a waltz where no party knew the steps.

She searched her mind for something—anything—to say that might draw warmth from him, some stimulated views but came up blank. Oh dear. This did not bode well for either of them. If they had already run out of conversational topics now, however would they last years of marriage...

"Being outside beneath the stars," she tried again softly, "is it not romantic?" Surely that would turn his thoughts to the possibility of a kiss. Of moving them away from the guests who stood nearby and give them privacy.

Instead, he shrugged, staring out at the lawns as though he had never seen grass before. "Shall we return indoors? I do not wish you to be missed by the duke and duchess."

Disappointment stabbed at her that he seemed far from agreeable, and somewhat cold to how he had been at previous events. Return indoors? What gentleman would wish to return indoors when such an opportunity arose?

"Of course," she said quietly, not seeing the point in dallying outside a moment longer.

She started back without taking his arm, feeling a sting of disappointment at his lack of interest. Her cheeks burned, though whether from humiliation or frustration she could not say. The music drifted faintly from the ballroom, a bright, laughing tune at odds with the heavy ache settling in her chest.

She could not help but think that, had it been Whitmore at her side on a darkened terrace—well, not entirely dark, nor devoid of people, but private enough—he would have seen the opportunity before him and taken advantage of it. The duke, however, seemed eager to return her to her family as quickly as possible.

They stepped back into the ballroom, where light and sound rushed to meet them. The air was thick with warmth and perfume, the swirl of dancers moving in time to a country reel. The duke escorted her back to where Ravensmere and Rosalind stood. After a brief exchange of pleasantries, he excused himself and was gone.

Isabella watched him retreat into the crowd,

utterly flummoxed by his demeanor. Was he not supposed to have danced with her? Whatever had happened to that promise?

She snapped her fan open, more from agitation than grace. She could not deem his behavior anything other than flippant. Were all men so capricious?

As if her very thought of unreliable men conjured the embodiment of that term, the Marquess of Whitmore entered the ballroom.

The shift in the space was immediate. Conversations of the female kind faltered, heads turned. The light caught the dark gloss of his hair as he made his addresses to their host this evening. His gaze swept across the crowd with practiced ease—commanding, amused, far too confident for a man who had no right to be as handsome as he was.

She straightened her shoulders, rallying herself for whatever the night would bring. The violins struck up another waltz, slow and alluring as she fixed her gaze on the marquess. He would come to her—she had no doubt—and when he did, she would see if he were as erratic as the duke.

She ignored the small hope blossoming inside of her that he would prove otherwise.

CHAPTER ELEVEN

Hartley had watched Lady Isabella and the Duke of Rolle re-enter the ballroom. The duke had looked ashen. Desperation all but written across his features, as though he could not be rid of Lady Isabella quickly enough. He returned her to Ravensmere and the duchess, speaking hurriedly before taking a bow and leaving as promptly as he had arrived.

Hartley tracked his progress through the crowded room, noting the quick pace and stiff posture. Curiosity got the better of him and he followed, wanting to speak to him about what had transpired outside on the terrace.

He caught up to Rolle before he joined a group of their mutual friends. "Rolle," he called, his tone low but firm. "What happened on the terrace?" he asked when he was closer and sure no one was listening to their conversation.

There were games afoot and he was determined to get to the bottom of them. If Rolle had won the bet, he needed to know. He ground his teeth at the thought, putting his annoyance down to losing a thousand pounds and not the jealousy he feared it may be instead.

Rolle regarded those nearby. Seeking assurance of their privacy he lowered his voice. "Nothing occurred. But not without Lady Isabella's considerable attempt to alter that outcome."

A cold chill ran down Whitmore's spine. His hands stilled at his sides, and he fought not to clasp the duke's lapels and demand and answer. The noise of the ballroom dimmed beneath the sudden rush of blood in his ears. "What are you saying?"

Not that he particularly wished to know if Lady Isabella was more inclined toward the duke than him. He told himself his concern stemmed solely from the wager—and he never lost. Yet a deep, unwelcome thought stirred. Perhaps, in this case, he did care.

A first for him.

"I do believe that Lady Isabella," the duke continued, "was attempting to lead me away from the crowd on the terrace to... How shall I say it? To experience her first kiss."

Whitmore's jaw tightened. He pursed his lips, fighting the urge to not let the information discompose him. He could almost see her in his mind's eye, standing beneath the terrace lanterns, her hair catching the moonlight, her lips parted in expectation. The image struck him with an uncomfortable force.

"You must be mistaken," he said at last. "Lady Isabella is the daughter of a duke. She would not act so fast or reckless no matter our attempts to make her do otherwise."

Certainly she had not done so with him. A pity,

perhaps, for he could see himself kissing her—and enjoying that pastime exceedingly well. The thought of her soft mouth beneath his own, the faint tremble of her breath, sent an unwelcome heat through his blood.

He shook the thought aside. It was not helpful.

"She was quite flirtatious," the duke replied evenly, "and I am not so certain we should continue with this bet. I have since met someone... A Miss Wilson from Bath, and I do believe I like her more than anyone I have encountered in society these past years. I would not wish to lead Lady Isabella on, nor allow her to develop feelings that will not be returned."

Hartley narrowed his eyes. "Now you have a conscience and are worried about hurting her female heart?"

"I was foxed when I suggested the bet. You should not have accepted it."

He should not have, but he didn't need to be told such a thing, especially from Rolle. Who the hell did he think he was? "So I'm to blame for this farce?" he stated.

"Well, no..." the duke stammered.

Hartley sighed. "So, I win the bet, and you owe me one thousand pounds."

The duke held up his hand, wagging a finger. "Nay, you have not won her hand yet—whether I am involved or not. And since she has shown a liking for me, it does not seem likely that you will succeed. So you shall continue this wager alone and we shall see if you are bestowed a kiss from her."

Whitmore arched a brow, masking irritation behind a lazy smile. "Very well, the game remains.

And if you prefer Miss Wilson, by all means, pursue her. I am more than willing to double my money at your expense."

"We shall see whether the Marquess of Whitmore is as roguish and tempting enough to the fair Lady Isabella."

"Oh, you shall see," Whitmore added, his grin widening. "My reputation speaks for itself and I shall not fail wooing her."

The duke smirked. "I think Lady Isabella will be more of a challenge than you believe. She seemed quite determined earlier if I'm to read between her fluttering eyes and pouty mouth. I do not think she likes you in that way and prefers me instead."

Hartley could tell the duke was riling him up, deliberately provoking his ego to gain a reaction. He was trying to see how far he could push before Whitmore lost his temper—or worse, cut him dead in society.

He would not take the bait.

"You are lucky we are friends," Whitmore said, his tone cool, "else I might take offense at that remark. But I will overlook it and you shall see, Your Grace. I will win her first kiss—and whatever else she might be inclined to bestow."

A spark of mischief lit within him, though beneath it simmered something deeper, something he refused to name. The thrill of pursuit no longer felt like a simple wager. Oh no, it had begun to stir unease he could not quite dispel.

"I would wish you success, but then, that would mean I would be a thousand pounds poorer, so I shall keep those sentiments to myself."

Hartley chuckled. "A kiss does not need to mean

anything more than what it is," he murmured almost absently, "Lady Isabella will come to realize that universal truth."

The duke smirked. "I fear your confidence will be your undoing."

"I will relieve you of the wager soon enough," Whitmore said, his tone deceptively light. "You will see, by the end of the Season, that one thousand pounds will be mine."

"Well then," the duke replied, adjusting his cuffs. "If you will excuse me, I see Miss Wilson across the room and I wish to speak with her."

Whitmore inclined his head. "Good luck to you, too."

He watched the duke depart, a smug smile curving his lips. The orchestra had struck up another set, violins and flutes weaving through the hum of voices. Candlelight shimmered off crystal chandeliers, scattering tiny sparks of gold across the polished parquetry floor.

For a long moment, he remained where he was, the crowd swirling about him in a blur of color and gaiety. Then his gaze swept the ballroom, searching.

Lady Isabella stood near the far wall beside her sister and brother-in-law, her posture graceful, her fan moving in slow, deliberate arcs. The pale silk of her gown caught the candlelight, the faint shimmer of silver thread gliding like moonlight across water. Her laughter, soft yet vibrant, reached him even through the din of the crowd. It struck him squarely in the chest.

He took a steadying breath and rallied himself.

Indeed. She would be his, and if not tonight, then soon.

Very soon.

Hartley started in her direction, weaving through clusters of guests with effortless charm. The murmurs of the *ton* followed him—admiring glances, whispered remarks, a few jealous sighs. He was used to such attention, wore it like armor. But tonight, for reasons he could not quite explain, it felt heavier than usual.

His smile sharpened. He could almost taste the anticipation in the air, the charged hum between hunter and prey. Lady Isabella Ravensmere might not know it yet, but their little game was far from over.

And he intended to win.

CHAPTER TWELVE

Isabella felt extremely foolish and embarrassed after how she had behaved on the terrace. She swallowed the bile that rose in her throat at the thought of what she had hinted to the duke to do with her.

How could she act so foolish? So reckless or fast?

She could only hope he would not go about society and tell people of her atrocious behavior—of her trying to get him to bestow a kiss upon her when such a thing was absolutely inappropriate.

Surely, he would not.

She hadn't actually asked for him to kiss her. Inferring was one thing, but he would not be so cruel as to spread gossip. To do so would degrade her name, and in the process, make him look immoral as well.

And he was not a cruel person. She was certain of that, even if perhaps his interest in her had waned and he no longer wished to pursue her.

She tried to stop herself from panicking and

moved to stroll about the room, sipping her ratafia, and forcing herself to think of something else. The music swelled around her, the steady hum of conversation rising and falling beneath the waltz's rhythm. Candlelight flickered off the mirrors lining the room, throwing soft golden light over everyone.

Whitmore was now at the ball. She had spied him a time or two—even once speaking with Rolle. She wished she knew what they were discussing.

She could only hope it was not her.

She stopped near the ballroom entrance doors that opened into the foyer. Standing alone she watched as couples swept past her in a blur of color and laughter. The air was warm and thick with perfume.

Her stomach wavered uneasily as she watched the dancers, their faces flushed with wine and delight. The sight only reminded her how very reckless she had been.

Finishing her glass of ratafia, she handed the empty crystal to a passing footman and stepped quietly away. She strolled along an empty passageway, remembering that this house had a marvelous conservatory.

But before she could reach it, she heard voices.

She paused, head tilting, trying to gauge which room the exchange came from. A sliver of lamplight spilled across the floor from a door left slightly ajar, and the faint cadence of a man's voice—low and rich—drifted through.

A warning voice in her head told her to turn back, to return to the ballroom and ignore whatever was unfolding within the house. Balls and parties always hid their share of indiscretions. It was better for one to not involve oneself into situations that were not hers to start with.

Still, she had been rather naughty this evening already. A small part of her—reckless and stung by humiliation—wanted to revel in the knowledge that others might be equally scandalous.

She approached the door and placed her ear against it. She heard a man and a woman within, the low murmur of intimate conversation. She closed her eyes, shame washing through her when she recognised who conversed.

The Duke of Rolle.

And Miss Wilson.

She froze at what the exchange entailed.

"I did not think you were interested in me, Your Grace," Miss Wilson said, her sweet yet vulnerable words floating to where Isabella stood.

"I cannot be obvious with whom I wish to court, Miss Wilson," the duke returned. "But it is you I would like to know better—if you are open to such a courtship."

"I am more than willing, Your Grace," came the eager reply.

Isabella stepped back from the door as if struck. She would not listen further. She would not intrude.

But what was the meaning of this?

Only yesterday—indeed, only an hour ago—the duke had seemed fully engaged with her. Was he no better than so many other gentlemen of society, playing with young ladies' affections merely for amusement until someone more convenient caught their eye? She could only calculate from what she heard that he indeed was no different.

And here she was but moments ago thinking he was kind. That he was honorable and truthful with his courting of her.

How silly and green she was to have thrown herself at his head. After his conversation with Miss Wilson, it was any wonder he fled. He did not like her, and he certainly didn't wish to kiss her.

Heat burned across her cheeks, shame crawling down her neck like a rash. The memory of her attempt at flirtation—the words, the look she'd given him—now seemed mortifyingly transparent.

Isabella fled, hurrying toward the conservatory. Her slippers made no sound on the tiled flood, but her breath came unevenly, loud in her ears. She prayed no one saw her flight. She needed air—space to think—to let the degradation ebb before she faced anyone again.

Inside the conservatory, the world was blessedly quiet. The scent of night-blooming jasmine filled the air, mingling with damp earth and the faint metallic tang of glass cooled by the night.

She moved toward the great glass window that overlooked the gardens, staring at her reflection caught in the faint light from the adjoining hall. Her pale face, wide eyes, and trembling hands stared back at her.

"Fool," she whispered under her breath. She closed her eyes and drew in a steadying breath.

The sound of a boot and movement behind her startled her. She turned only to see the one man she did not wish to face. Not when she was feeling far too vulnerable.

"Whitmore," she said, her voice devoid of feeling. "What are you doing here?" Her tone sounded bored—she hoped it sounded wearied even if her heart jumped at the sight of him—and she prayed he would take the hint and leave her alone.

"You looked distraught leaving the ball," he said softly. "I wanted to check on you?"

"I'm well," she replied. No, that was not true. She was mortified, and his presence only made it worse. "Please leave me alone." She turned to look back outside.

He ignored her plea and came to stand beside her. In the reflection of the window, she saw him watching her. The lamplight caught in his dark hair, the fine line of his jaw, his expression unreadable but not unkind. His closeness unsettled her far more than she cared to admit.

"You know of the duke and Miss Wilson," he stated quietly.

Her head snapped up. "You know of them?"

He nodded. "He mentioned it tonight. We are friends after all."

She turned away, hugging her arms around herself. "I am not injured, if that is what you're wondering." Not entirely true. Her pride was, but in truth her heart was untouched. A small mercy she granted.

"Then what are you?" he asked.

She could feel his gaze on her cheek, warm and steady, but she could not look at him. Her throat tightened.

"I threw myself at him earlier this evening," she said in a rush. "But had I known he liked Miss Wilson, I would never have done so. I do not even know why I did it. I'm not charmed of him in that way in the first place."

"Good to know."

She continued, now that she was stating her shame, she could not stop. "The duke is a kind and well-mannered man—or so I thought—but I do not desire him as one should."

Whitmore was silent, clearly taking in her words.

"You threw yourself at him?" he murmured, almost amused. "But you do not desire him? I think I'm confused."

"I wished to see," she admitted. "If he was sincere in his attentions. It seems he has failed abysmally like so many before him. For any man who truly desired a woman would have kissed her, yes?"

"A man would indeed kiss the woman he desired," he said quietly.

Her breath caught. "Not that I should be speaking to you about this. But considering you and I are practically related—"

"We are not related," he interrupted. "My brother is married to your sister. That does not make us family."

"Even so, I am certain my secrets are safe with you. Even if you are a rogue."

"They are indeed," he said, his voice rougher than before.

His promise made her feel strangely steadier. "It just does not make sense to me." She frowned down at a nearby fern. "Why the duke, these past several days, has sought me out—dancing, conversing—

only to turn about and court another. What am I to make of that?"

Whitmore reached up and adjusted his cravat. "Perhaps he's merely had a change of heart, my lady?"

She arched a brow. "A change of heart? How fickle if that is the case." She paused. "And what is this *my lady* business, Whitmore? What happened to calling me Bells?"

He grinned, and she hated that warmth spiraled through her.

"I didn't think you liked me calling you Bells."

"I don't," she lied. And that was the rub—she did like it. It sounded intimate and forbidden. The way his voice softened over the word. It stirred something dangerous in her she'd not known before.

Perhaps her attempt at kissing the duke had been her way of distracting herself from something else entirely. What Whitmore truly made her feel.

But she could not ask him if him being here meant more than trying to console a friend. She could not tempt him as she had the duke. For what if she kissed Whitmore—and it was everything she had ever imagined? Perfect in every sense. What then?

She did not like Whitmore. He was aggravating and pompous and far too handsome for his own good. Still...as she looked up at him she couldn't help but wonder what it might feel like to be kissed by the marquess.

Truly kissed. A toe curling in your slipper kind of kiss...

The thought lingered in the quiet between

them, heavy and unspoken. Outside, a soft rain began to fall, the droplets tapping gently against the conservatory glass. The sound filled the silence like a heartbeat, slow and rhythmic, as her pulse raced to match it.

Kissing the marquess, she couldn't help but believe, would be wonderful.

CHAPTER
THIRTEEN

Hartley debated whether he should lean down and kiss those very desirable lips. Of course he could not. There were people about. The house was hosting a ball for heaven's sake, filled with too many eyes. He could not be so bold — not with a woman who was unmarried and very much a maid.

He held out his arm instead, determined to act the gentleman, if only once in his life.

"Shall we return to the ball?"

He could see the confusion flicker in her eyes. She had perhaps expected a different response from him — hoped for one, even. So had he, but there were rules to being a rogue. And kissing a woman who was unmarried and untouched in a glass conservatory where anyone may be watching was not it.

"I thank you. Yes," she said softly.

They walked back to the ballroom in silence, their footsteps quiet on the marble floor, the distant strains of music growing louder as they neared the room. The faint scent of beeswax drifted through the corridor, mingling with the warmth of the candlelight. Isabella's gloved hand rested lightly on his arm, and though the contact was innocent, it seemed to burn through the fabric of his coat.

Thankfully, they passed no one who would question where they had been.

They re-entered the entertainment and Whitmore sensed the slight shift in the air — a few curious glances, the whisper of fans, a smattering of speculation that always followed him around like a cloak.

He returned her promptly to Ravensmere and the duchess's side.

"I am to ride in the park tomorrow morning," he said lightly, standing a few paces away but keeping his gaze on her.

Her eyes met his, a spark of surprise mingling with curiosity. "I'm due to ride in the park tomorrow morning as well, my lord. Perhaps I shall see you there."

"We could meet," he suggested, his mouth curving into a smile. "Or perhaps we should make it that we do. I know you are fond of riding, and I shall be trying out my new mare tomorrow. I recently purchased her from Tattersalls."

"Indeed?" She looked up at him with genuine interest, and he found himself oddly pleased by her attentiveness. The glow from the chandeliers above glinted against her dark hair, and he marveled at how beautiful she was. How was it that she was not betrothed or married for years? Such a prize should not be sitting on the proverbial wallflower shelf.

"Do you have many horses in your stable?" she asked.

"I have four in town," he replied, "and likely three times that number at the estate in Kent. I'm breeding them, you see — trying to secure strong bloodlines for racing. I hope to win at Ascot one day."

"That is interesting," she said. "I did not know you were so well acquainted with the racing industry. You continue to surprise me, Whitmore."

He grinned, silently pleased by her kind words. It was uncommon for her to speak to him in such a tone — without barbs, without suspicion. The warmth of it settled somewhere deep in his chest, where he was not accustomed to feeling anything at all.

There had been a time, long past, when there were few words exchanged between them — and none of them kind. Not that he hadn't tried to make her like him, but there was, it seemed, something inherently annoying about him she could not abide.

Perhaps she was thawing toward him at last. And it would certainly help him win that wager. A thousand pounds was no small sum — worthy enough to pursue.

"I always wished to breed horses," she said, glancing away. "At one time father had a fine collection of bloodlines in the stables, but he sold them."

It did not surprise Whitmore that the late Duke of Ravensmere had done so. The man had enjoyed nothing more than cards, claret, and scandal. Rumor — and Benedict's confirmation — held that it was only the current duke who had restored the family's finances and made his wards heiresses again.

"Perhaps one day you will have your own breeding program, Bells," he whispered. "Something tells me you would make a most astute businesswoman."

A small smile touched her lips. "Perhaps," she said softly. The candlelight caught in her eyes, turning them to liquid amber, and he had to look away before he forgot himself entirely.

The more time he spent in her company, the less he wished his courting had begun as a wager — a lark between friends. He could not shake the feeling that had he courted her in truth, they might have suited rather well. Possibly too well.

"If I do not marry, I could try to persuade Rosalind to convince the duke to allow me to begin a breeding program at Ebonmere Abbey. Although I presume they do not wish for me to live there forever, but if I do not marry, it is something to consider." She smiled faintly. "I could always move into one of the unused wings of the house. I would not be in anyone's way there."

Whitmore frowned, the notion irking him more than he cared to admit. The image of her tucked away in some quiet corner of the estate — alone, forgotten — stirred something sharp in his chest.

"I do not think your sister or brother-in-law would ever see you as being in the way," he said. "Should you not marry, they would welcome you for all of your days."

She laughed softly, though there was little humor in it. "I only mean that they have their own lives now — their family and plans. I would not wish to intrude."

"And with the Duke of Rolle no longer interested in courting me," she added bitterly, "my chances of making my third Season a success are diminishing by the minute."

"Come now," he said, his tone gentling. "Let us not be melancholy. It is not in your nature." He wiggled his brow, and at last she smiled — truly smiled — the expression lighting up her face.

Hell she was beautiful...

"You are right," she said with a laugh. "And I am riding with Lord Whitmore tomorrow in the park, do you know. That will make me the envy of many young ladies."

He cleared his throat, sensing her bantering was coming back. "Would it make you envious, were you not the one riding with me tomorrow? If you were one of those young ladies looking on from afar, wishing it was them that I talk to, that my eyes linger upon..."

Her laughter, carefree and bright, washed over him like warm sunlight. The sound sank beneath his skin, earnest and intoxicating. For a man so used to laughter at his expense, hearing hers felt like a victory.

"If I longed for you to be my husband, perhaps," she teased, "but we are merely friends. Are we not?"

He inclined his head. "We are indeed." And yet, the words felt hollow as they left his mouth.

As the orchestra struck the opening notes of another dance, he found himself watching her — the graceful curve of her neck as she turned to speak to her sister, the delicate flush on her cheeks that came from enjoyment rather than shame. Her presence filled the air around him, and he could not quite catch his breath.

If friendship were all they shared, then why did it feel as though something beneath it simmered quietly, waiting for the slightest spark?

She caught his gaze, her smile softening. For a moment, the crowded ballroom faded — the glittering chandeliers, the rustle of satin, the murmuring *ton* all dissolved into distant sound.

All he could see was her.

And perhaps, he thought fleetingly, if fortune had dealt his life a different hand, he might have been foolish enough to fall.

CHAPTER FOURTEEN

By the time Isabella had arrived at the park the following morning, Whitmore was already waiting for her.

He sat tall astride his horse, looking out over the wide expanse of green. The morning mist still clung to the grass, and sunlight broke weakly through a veil of clouds, casting soft light over the dewy ground. His silhouette, proud and still, seemed carved into the damp air — the image of a man lost in thought.

She told her groom to wait for her at the end of the Row and pushed her mount forward. The rhythmic sound of hooves against wet gravel carried to where he stood. Whitmore turned at her approaching, a smile spreading across his handsome face.

She shouldn't think of him in such a way of course. He was a rogue — a man who, from the moment she had met him, had been nothing short of a pebble in her silk slippers. Irritating, handsome, insufferably charming — or so he thought — the sort of man one ought to despise but never quite managed to.

Still, over the last few weeks, they had formed a truce. Perhaps even a friendship, as he had declared. Perchance things had changed between them, though she would not dare admit it aloud, she found the modification agreeable.

Whether courting or friendship, whatever this peculiar arrangement might be, he was making her Season more enjoyable than any she had endured before. The last two had been exercises in disappointment and tedium, full of forced smiles and false laughter. But now, with Whitmore's teasing remarks and unpredictable nature, she found herself smiling for reasons she could not quite define.

No matter how it ended, he had made this year better than the preceding one. And last night, when she had confessed her worry of being in her sister's way once they returned to Hampshire, he had spoken with a surprising gentleness — a side of him she had not expected. He had tried to ease her fears, had shown kindness instead of mockery.

For that, she would be forever grateful.

"Lady Isabella," he said now, using her full name with faux solemnity.

She pulled her mount to a stop beside him, her gaze sweeping over the mare he had spoken of so fondly the evening before.

"Good morning, my lord," she said. Her gaze drank in the sight of his muscled thighs before inspecting the horse. The mare was exquisite — sleek, chestnut-golden, her mane dark and shining even beneath the morning light. Whitmore's hand rested loosely on the reins, his posture one of easy control.

"She is a beauty," Isabella said. "And she seems placid enough. What is she like to ride?"

"She can be fiery," he admitted, urging his horse into a slow walk. "But nothing I cannot handle."

"I have a stallion at home now," she said as they moved side by side. "He's from good breeding stock, but very placid in nature. Even around mares, he doesn't so much as lift his head."

"Then he is a rare sort," Whitmore said, glancing at her. "Perhaps he would suit for breeding with my mare — should you move forward with that program we discussed."

She smiled at the suggestion. "I would like that. I should very much like to see him cover a mare of her quality. He's from the Darley line — his sire came second at Ascot."

"Better and better." A spark lit his dark eyes, genuine interest warming his tone. "You know more about breeding than most gentlemen I meet in Tattersalls."

"I have an interest, but I'm no expert," she said with quiet modesty. "Though I'm certain the little knowledge I do hold isn't looked upon as ladylike."

"Ladylike or not it's an admirable quality, to me at least. You have a mind for business as well as pleasure. A rare combination, Bells."

She looked away, trying not to show how much his words pleased her. "You flatter me, my lord."

"Only when it's deserved," he said easily.

They continued along the path, the gentle clop of their horses' hooves echoing through the park.

Few riders were out this morning. The trees swayed in the growing breeze, and a cool dampness hung in the air, as though the weather were holding its breath.

Whitmore's gaze lingered on her profile. "You seem lost in thought," he said. "Did I bore you with talk of women's admirable qualities?"

"Not at all," she replied. "I was thinking how different you are when you speak of horses. It's almost sincere."

He gave a mock gasp. "You wound me, Lady Isabella. Are you implying I am not always sincere or serious?"

She arched a brow at him. "Clearly, only when you wish to be."

He laughed softly. "Touché."

His chuckle rippled through her, unexpected and warm. She turned her face away so he would not see the smile tugging at her lips. A clap of thunder rumbled faintly in the distance, cutting through her amusement.

Isabella looked up at the sky. "It seems we're about to have a storm," she said, frowning. "I should probably return home."

He followed her gaze, his brow furrowing. "It was fine only moments ago. How strange."

"London weather is a fickle creature."

"Indeed," he said, glancing toward the horizon. "We may outrun it if we turn back now—"

Before either could move, the first drops of rain splattered against Isabella's hand. She stilled, hoping it would pass. Instead, the heavens opened.

The rain fell in earnest — thick, heavy drops

that soaked through her jacket and skirts and dampened her riding hat in seconds.

"Oh dear heavens," she gasped, laughing despite herself. "We shall be drenched!"

"Come!" he called, turning his mare about. "There — the copse of trees!"

Isabella followed, urging her horse after his. The cold rain lashed her face, her skirts clinging to her legs. The scent of wet earth and crushed grass rose sharply around them. The rhythmic pound of hooves against the soaked ground mingled with the steady roar of the downpour.

Under the trees, they found relative shelter. The thick foliage caught much of the rain, though drops still fell intermittently through the leaves. They sat side by side, watching the storm pummel the park beyond.

"This is torrential indeed," Whitmore said, shaking his head.

"Yes," she replied, brushing damp curls from her temple. "It's as if the heavens themselves are displeased with us."

"Or perhaps they're merely testing our resolve."

"To what purpose?" she asked.

"To see whether we can sit together in polite company without scandal," he said, eyes glinting.

"Then we are doomed," she said, trying not to laugh. "For we forever do not."

A gust of wind picked up, and she shivered. Whitmore noticed immediately and shifted closer. He reached out, his arm settling gently around her shoulders.

She ought to have pulled away, to remind him it was improper. But with no one in sight and the rain pressing close, she said nothing. The warmth of his arm seeped through the damp fabric of her gown, his hand rubbing lightly over her sleeve in a wordless effort to warm her.

"I'm sorry I pressed for us to meet this morning. The storm will pass soon," he said quietly. "Then I shall escort you home."

"You weren't to know it would rain," she murmured. "You needn't apologize."

She looked up at him then — really looked — and saw that his own riding coat was soaked through, his dark hair curling damply against his brow. Droplets ran down his cheek and over the strong line of his jaw. One clung to his lower lip before falling, and she could not tear her gaze away.

Had she not thought him handsome before, she certainly did now. Handsome and desirable.

"Lady Isabella," he said softly.

"Hmm?"

"You're staring," he teased.

Her cheeks warmed. "I was not."

"You were." His voice was low, almost tender. "And I thank you for it."

She turned her face away, pretending to study the rain beyond the trees. "You are incorrigible."

"So I've been told."

A moment of silence stretched between them. The rain beat down heavily on the canopy above, the rhythmic patter oddly soothing.

He shifted closer still. She could feel the heat of his body beside hers, the faint brush of his breath against her temple. The world beyond the trees faded — all that remained was the sound of rain, the scent of wet leather and soap, and the steady thrum of her own pulse.

"You are quiet," he said after a while.

"I was thinking," she whispered.

"About what?"

"About how ridiculous we must look," she said, smiling faintly. "Hiding under a tree like a pair of foolish children."

"Better foolish than cold," he said.

"Perhaps." She hesitated, then added softly, "Or perhaps not."

He tilted his head. "Why not?"

"Because foolishness can lead to trouble." Trouble like her throwing herself at his head when she knew she should not.

"Ah," he murmured, his gaze dropping to her lips. "And do you fear trouble, my lady?"

"Yes."

"Liar," he said gently.

Her breath caught. "Hartley..."

"Hartley," he echoed, the word lingering in the air between them like a promise.

She had never spoken his given name aloud before. Hearing it now on her own lips felt intimate, forbidden. A warning. A plea.

"I'm going to kiss you now," Whitmore declared without guile.

The words should have sent her fleeing, should have made her draw away. But she did not move. She did not lift her reins or turn her horse.

Instead, she nodded — slow, inevitable — accepting her fate.

Accepting him.

The rain whispered through the leaves, a steady

hymn to the moment as he leaned closer. Her heart thundered in her chest, her breath caught between fear and anticipation. For the first time in her life, Lady Isabella Ravensmere did not think, did not weigh consequence or propriety.

She simply felt.

CHAPTER
FIFTEEN

You're in the park, you stupid fool. Anyone may be watching.

Still, it wasn't enough to stop him from kissing Isabella.

He cradled her face, tipped up her jaw and finally, sweet Jesus, finally kissed the woman who had haunted his every dream these past weeks. The kiss began as a soft coaxing of mouths, a joining of lips. He could tell she had never kissed a man before, but just as he had suspected, Isabella was quick to learn and was soon following his lead.

And of course, he led her toward sin. A place he knew well. She tasted as sweet as he had imagined — all deliciousness, and his to devour.

He cupped her face, sliding his hands into her damp hair, tipping her chin to deepen the kiss. Her hat fell back, her curls clinging to her cheeks from the rain, her breath catching in small, desperate gasps that drove him to madness.

She made a sweet, accepting murmur, and the sound went straight to his groin.

He groaned, wanting her with a fierceness that unsettled him — an urgency that rose from somewhere deeper than lust, something raw and uninvited.

There was something about kissing a woman who, until this very moment, had been so firmly against everything he stood for. They had been adversaries. Prickly acquaintances. Then, slowly, a truce. And now? Now he didn't know what to call them.

Enemies turned allies? Friends on the edge of folly? Lovers caught between propriety and ruin?

Whatever it was, it had undone him.

And he wanted more of it.

He couldn't imagine another night passing without kissing her again — without tasting her laughter, her warmth, her defiance, her soft gasp against his lips.

Her fingers fisted into the lapels of his coat, pulling him close, taking more than receiving. Somehow the kiss turned from sweet and coaxing to something wild and consuming — a tangle of breath and want, the sort of kiss that made the world fall away.

He pushed her, perhaps further than she was ready for, yet she met his experience with eagerness, with a natural response that left him all sixes and sevens — his body off balance, his mind spinning.

"Hartley," she gasped, breaking the kiss, his name a plea and a protest both.

He went to kiss her again, but the sound of approaching hooves brought him sharply back to his senses. He pulled away, looking up to see her groom riding toward them. The rain had ceased — when, he couldn't say.

He had been too lost in her.

"We must stop," he said quickly. "There's someone coming — your groom, I believe."

She straightened, fixing her hat and adjusting her skirts, her breath uneven.

He couldn't help but feel a flicker of annoyance — not at her, but at being interrupted. The air between them still crackled, alive with what they had done, with what might have been had the world not intruded.

"I've mussed your hair a little," he said, his voice low, rough. "Best fix it before he reaches us."

She moved to press several pins back into her coiffure. Within moments, she was once more the respectable Lady Isabella Ravensmere — cool, composed, untouchable.

He, however, felt anything but poised.

In fact, he had a terrible, crawling sense that the kiss had altered something within him — as though a locked door in his soul had been thrown wide open.

What it was, he could not yet name, but a gnawing ache settled in his gut at the thought of the woman before him not being his to kiss again whenever he wished.

You've all but won the bet. Tell the duke, claim your thousand pounds, and be done with her. Be rid of her. You weren't supposed to fall for her charms.

He rubbed a hand over his jaw, feeling the sting of self-loathing. He could still taste her on his lips, still feel the tremor in her breath against his cheek, and it shamed him.

He hated himself increasingly with every moment that passed. She would despise him if she ever discovered the truth — that their courtship, their friendship, this entire charade, had begun as a wager.

What had he been thinking? Other than being a fool at the time. Petty retaliation for her being snappish a the Kenworthy ball, her disdain of him on full display. A contempt observed by the Duke of Rolle. And now here he was, the fool undone by his own deceit.

"Is there anything you wish to ask me, my lord?"

Her question startled him. He looked at her, confused. "I do not believe so," he said, searching her expression and his mind on what she may expect. "Why do you ask?"

"You've kissed me, Whitmore."

He blinked. "I—yes, I suppose I have."

"You cannot say that is a normal thing for a gentleman to do," she said, her voice calm, steady. "Are you not going to marry me now?"

"Marry you?" The words burst from him before he could stop them. He nearly choked. "You think that I ought to ask you to marry me now?" Panic hit him, swift and sharp. His breath caught, his chest constricted. For a moment, he thought he might truly faint. He could still feel her lips beneath his, still hear that soft murmur, still want her — and the realization made him dizzy.

"It was only a kiss, Lady Isabella," he said finally, trying to sound composed. "I thought—well, when you mentioned the duke, and that you threw yourself at him, that it was something you wished to...experience. I was merely—"

Her laugh cut him off.

He stared, utterly lost.

"I do not wish to marry you, Lord Whitmore," she said, her lips curving. "Any more than you wish to marry me. But I thank you for the kiss. I did enjoy it quite a lot."

His mouth opened and then closed.

"In fact," she added impishly. "I would not have thought the tongue could be so...sensual. But there you have it."

Her grin made him gape. "You are jesting," he asked faintly.

"Not at all." Amusement danced in her eyes. "I merely wanted to see you squirm. The panic on your handsome face was reward enough."

He exhaled, somewhere between a groan and a laugh. "You're a minx."

"But if you were any type of honorable gentleman," she said lightly, "of course you would have asked for my hand, instead of looking as though you'd swallowed a wasp."

He frowned, but she only shrugged, perfectly at ease. Her calm unsettled him far more than her anger would have. Did she not care at all? Perhaps she really did not. Perhaps she truly had no interest in him — beyond curiosity.

"I wanted to see," she said.

"To see what?"

"To see and to know," she replied. "Now I do."

"See and know what, Isabella?" Feeling his patience slip.

She tilted her head. "What has happened

here today merely confirms what I have always known. You're a veritable rake. A man who takes opportunities afforded to him and then rides off into the sunset, no matter the damage he leaves in his wake. You will never change, but at least I know your true self. A shame for I had started to think you may have finally matured."

"Matured?" he echoed, stung.

She straightened in her saddle, every inch the proud lady he knew her to be. "You need not seek me out at any more balls or parties. I shall not expect your company, nor shall I believe any further kindness from you is given with validity."

He shut his mouth with a snap, his mind furiously thinking of what to say. "I do enjoy spending time with you," he said finally, his voice rougher than he intended. "But perhaps your question threw me, that is all. It does not mean I am not ready for marriage." He paused, wondering where the hell that thought came from.

She raised her brows, lips curling in quiet triumph. "Do not fool yourself, my lord. It is not becoming."

"This—" he gestured helplessly between them "—has been enjoyable. It has..."

"I agree," she said. "And now it is finished. I really must return home. I imagine you'll be at the Hadon ball this evening?"

"I will," he said, though he could hardly remember agreeing to it or why she should care after her harsh words.

"I shall be in attendance also," she said, gathering her reins. "But I think it best if we do not speak." She turned her horse and rode off, meeting her groom halfway down the Row.

Hartley did not follow. He watched as she rode away, the hem of her riding habit darkened by the weather, her posture proud despite their conversation.

"Damn it," he muttered. He ran a hand through his hair. The scent of her — faint rose and rain — still lingered on his fingers, tormenting him.

He was such an ass. Sounded like one too. And she knew it.

But he was free now. He could go on with his Season, return to his lovers, drink, laugh, and forget her entirely. He'd kissed her. He could claim his blunt and be done with the stupid wager.

All should be well.

But as he sat there, the ache in his chest said otherwise. The thought of her laughter — of her clever, cutting words — haunted him. He had kissed her to win. Yet the feel of her lips had branded him like sin. Branded him as the property of hers.

"Damn it," he swore again. "What the hell was that?"

Because for the first time in his life, Whitmore realized he no longer knew what his next move would be, but bedamned it would involve them never speaking again. That was for sure.

CHAPTER SIXTEEN

Whitmore nursed a brandy at his usual table in White's the following evening. The heavy scent of cigars and old leather thick in the air. Rain continued to drizzle against the tall windows, the sound soft but relentless, a rhythm that seemed to echo his never-ending thoughts.

He had not slept well. Every time he closed his eyes, he felt Isabella's lips against his. Her soft sigh. The warmth of her hands. Her laughter afterward — teasing him, unbothered, while he sat there undone like some green boy after his first kiss.

"Ah, there you are," came the smooth drawl of the Duke of Rolle, striding toward him with his usual calm assurance. His boots shone, his coat pristine. A man untouched by self-doubt.

Whitmore wished he could say the same.

The duke dropped into the seat opposite and waved for a glass. "I had meant to seek you out sooner, but business delayed me. So, tell me," the duke settling into his chair. "Have you kissed her yet? I'll send you your thousand pounds by the week's end if you have."

Whitmore stared into his drink. "I don't want your money or any part of the stake Consider the bet null and void."

"Nonsense. A bet's a bet, and if you've fulfilled it, you shall be paid. So tell me, have you kissed Lady Isabella?"

He said nothing.

The duke smiled. "I'll take your silence as your attempt to protect the lady's virtue." He paused, thanking a footman for his glass of brandy. "However, you appear as though victory doesn't suit you."

"Perhaps it doesn't," Whitmore muttered, setting down his glass. "Perhaps I've begun to tire of risks when they are at others expense."

The duke's brow arched. "A strange confession from a man who up until now has thrived on it."

"Even a fox grows weary of the chase when he finds he's cornered himself," Whitmore said, too low hopefully for the duke to hear. He didn't need his fellow peer to know how he suffered or laugh at him for being melancholy.

"Come now, Whitmore, don't be maudlin. You've done nothing wrong. Lady Isabella's pride will survive, and you've earned yourself a tidy sum."

He forced a smirk. "You make it sound so noble, but you're wrong. She's not injured at all. In fact, I do not think she could care a tidbit about what we did," he admitted, wanting to rip back the words as soon as he'd uttered them. And that was the rub, was it not? Her easy dismissal of him. The only woman in London who refused to succumb to his charms, even after a kiss.

What the hell was wrong with him? Had he lost his ability to seduce the fairer sex?

The duke chuckled and signaled for the waiter. "You'll feel better after a few hands of cards tonight."

Whitmore didn't answer. His attention had shifted to the table behind them, where two younger peers were laughing over their own brandies.

"She's a rare beauty," one said — Lord Lennox, a fellow known for his good manners and better breeding. "I noticed her at the ball last night. Stunning eyes. Carries herself like a duchess, which isn't surprising considering she's a duke's daughter, though I hear she's still unmarried."

"Three Seasons, is it not?" his companion stated.

"Aye. A spinster by society's cruel measure. Which makes her ripe for the plucking."

The man's laugh grated across Whitmore's nerves. They had to be speaking of Bells.

"I mean to make a consorted effort for her hand," Lord Lennox continued. "Her dowry's handsome, her connections excellent, and she deserves better than to be overlooked. I shall call on Ravensmere next week."

Whitmore's jaw tightened. He told himself it was of no concern to him. That she was free to marry whomever she pleased. That he had no claim. But the thought of another man touching her, kissing her, made his chest twist painfully.

"You've gone pale," the duke said, studying him.

"I'm fine," Whitmore said shortly.

"Are you?"

"Only bored." He pushed back his chair and tossed a few coins on the table. "If you'll excuse me, I've a meeting with my steward."

"At this hour?" The duke frowned but said nothing further, letting him go.

Whitmore left the club without looking back, the murmur of the other men's conversation chasing him out into the misty evening. The city smelled of wet stone and carriage smoke. His thoughts churned, restless, ugly things he could neither silence nor justify.

Sleep was what he needed. All would be well by morning. He'd be back to his usual, assured self and all thoughts of a pretty brunette would cease in his mind.

The Romley ball the following evening was in full swing by the time he arrived — much later than intended thanks to his dallying at home. His meeting with his steward had stretched long into the afternoon, and by the time he'd exchanged his coat for formal attire and stepped into the grand hall of Lord and Lady Romley's, the ball was already half over.

He took in the scene before him, the dancers and those in attendance. Ice ran through his blood when his gaze settled on one particular, very comely chit.

He narrowed his eyes. Lady Isabella was waltzing. And not with some doddering peer or overeager puppy, but with Lord Lennox, the very man from White's the night before.

Whitmore's stomach knotted as he watched them all but float across the floor. Isabella was radiant — her gown a pale-blue silk that shimmered with each step, her cheeks flushed, her smile bright. She looked happy. Too happy.

Lord Lennox held her with an easy grace, his hand respectful but firm at her waist. The man was decent. Kind. A good family. No debts, no scandal, no mistress tucked away in Mayfair. In short, everything Whitmore was not.

He clenched his fists at his sides and even though he knew he ought to look away, to save himself from watching what was clearly unfolding before him, he could not.

Isabella glanced up mid-turn and saw him standing there. For one heart-stopping second, their gazes locked. Her smile did not falter — in fact, it deepened, just slightly. The smug tilt of her lips said she knew exactly what she was doing.

"God help me," he muttered under his breath.

When the waltz ended, Isabella curtsied gracefully, her laughter light as Lord Lennox said something in her ear that she found amusing. Whitmore didn't wait. As soon as her partner bowed and drifted away, he crossed the room.

"Lady Isabella," he said, too evenly and curt.

She turned, her fan fluttering lazily in her hand. "Lord Whitmore."

"You seem to be enjoying yourself."

"Why should I not?" Her tone was all sweetness, but there was a steel in her gaze that told him she was wishing him elsewhere, but too well bred to say it before anyone nearby. "It is a delightful evening. The music is divine, and my partners this evening have been most agreeable."

"I see." He took a step closer. "Lord Lennox, was it?" He hated that he sounded put out, jealous as hell. He'd kissed her for a bet, what the hell was he doing even standing at the Romley ball demanding to know what she was doing with another man. What was it to him what she got up to?

"Indeed. A most charming gentleman."

"Yes, I've heard he is." He ground his teeth and fought for calm.

Her brow lifted. "You've heard of him?"

"We are acquainted."

"Then you'll be pleased to know he is recently returned from Italy. Quite the traveler."

"So I hear," he said, his voice tight. The music swelled around them — a bright reel — but for Whitmore the sound blurred to a dull roar. All he saw was her. All he smelled was her perfume — rose and something warmer, softer, that clung to his memory like sin.

"I had not realized you favored gentlemen with impeccable manners and modest habits," he said. "It is any wonder we did not suit?"

"I find I favor gentlemen who are honest," she said, her smile unwavering.

He flinched. "And you think I am not?" And why would she not think so? He'd played her the fool. It was only luck that she did not know the full truth of his deception, or she would not even now be speaking to him.

"Do you?" she returned quietly.

He hesitated. "Bells—"

"Lady Isabella," she corrected gently.

He exhaled. "You intend to make me insane, do you not? I think after what happened in the park we need to speak privately."

Her fan stilled. "You flatter yourself if you think I'm going anywhere with you, my lord."

He glanced around. No one was near. They stood partially concealed by a tall, potted palm, the guests nearby too busy with their own amusements to concern themselves with their doings.

"Tell me," he said, his tone low, "what game are you playing?"

"No game, my lord. I am simply dancing. Laughing when something amuses me. Living my best life until I return to Hampshire or marry."

"And you think to marry Lord Lennox."

"Should it matter to you?"

"No," he said too quickly, hating that it did matter. He loathed the very idea of her being held, kissed, even looked upon if it were anyone but him. Damn, he was a fool and acting like one. Whatever had happened to him? Somehow after one kiss he'd turned into a desperate husk of his past self.

Her eyes sparkled with amusement. "You sound defensive."

"I am not."

"You are jealous," she said simply.

He stiffened, hating the fact that her barb had hit him squarely in the chest and unfortunately, was not incorrect. "I am not jealous." Oh, but he was. Maddeningly so.

"You are."

"Am not."

"You most certainly are," she said, her fan snapping shut. "And it's rather unbecoming, my lord. Especially for a man who once told me he could not bear the idea of marriage."

"That was before," he began, then stopped himself. Before what? Before he'd kissed her? Before she'd undone him with a single smile? With her touch. The feel of her pliant, sweet body in his arms.

"Before you kissed me?" she supplied, her brows raised mockingly.

He met her gaze, the challenge in her eyes impossible to ignore. "You presume too much."

"I presume exactly as much as you allow me to see. I'm rarely wrong, not when it comes to you, Whitmore."

Her words cut through the noise and laughter like a blade. He didn't know whether to curse her or kiss her.

So he did the latter.

He moved before he thought — one step forward, one hand sliding around her waist, pulling her back into the shadow of the palm. His mouth found hers before she could protest, before she could slap some sense back into his stupid head.

She gasped and he hoped she'd stop him. Push him away. She did neither.

At the touch of her lips, the kiss turned fierce, desperate — not a hesitant caress, fearful of those who may see. It was hungry, a fusing of mouths that fought to control the other. He tasted her desire, her outrage, her need — all tangled together, igniting him like kindling.

She should have pushed him away. He half-expected it. But instead, her fingers curled into the lapels of his coat and she kissed him back — a hungry gasp escaping her throat that made his cock hard.

Rock hard.

He broke away, breathing ragged. Her lips were flushed, her chest rising and falling in quick, uneven breaths. The sound of the orchestra reached them again — lilting, romantic, utterly oblivious to their ruin.

"Have you lost your mind?" she whispered, looking out past the ferns to see if anyone had seen them.

"Entirely."

"You will cause a scandal, and we will be forced to marry. That is not what either of us want."

"Do I not? Right at this moment being scandalous with you sounds sweet indeed."

"You cannot mean that."

He pressed his forehead to hers, closing his eyes. "I don't know what I mean anymore." For a long moment they stood there, caught between propriety and desire, the murmur of the ballroom just beyond the leaves. He should leave, but still his feet remained firmly planted in one spot.

"Why do you do this?" she asked softly. "You cannot decide if you hate me or desire me."

"Perhaps it's both," he said hoarsely.

"That is not flattering."

"Neither is honesty," he said, managing a wry smile. All he knew right at this moment is he wanted her, whether that was forever or for a night he could not say. But he did not want to leave her side. No need for monetary persuasion this time.

Her lips curved slightly. "You're impossible."

"And yet, you kissed me back and are still here. There is hope for us yet."

"I only allowed your kiss to make you stop talking."

He laughed quietly, but there was no humor in it. Inside, he was unmoored — torn between wanting to claim her and wanting to protect her from himself. He didn't want to hurt Isabella, but he had a sinking feeling that he would be a disappointment. The scandalous Lord Whitmore who always managed to get himself into trouble with the *ton*.

"I should leave," she said. "Before someone sees."

He nodded, though his hand still lingered at her waist. "Go, then."

She looked up at him one last time — eyes bright, unreadable — then turned and slipped back into the golden light of the ballroom, her gown whispering over the marble floor.

Whitmore remained hidden behind the palm, his pulse racing, his thoughts a storm. He could still feel the ghost of her lips on his, the taste of her laughter, the ache she left in her wake.

He was a fool.

A damned, lost fool.

And worse — he knew it.

CHAPTER
SEVENTEEN

The moment Whitmore's lips left hers, Isabella knew she had to flee.

Her heart thundered wildly beneath her ribs, her breath uneven, her skin still tingling from the press of his mouth. As she hastily pushed through the throng of guests, she could still feel the warmth of him, the rough whisper of his breath, the firm strength of his hands as they had drawn her near. It was madness — utter madness — to be thinking of him in such a way, and at a ball no less.

The ballroom around her seemed too bright, too loud — laughter and music blending into a dizzying hum that made her want to bolt. She turned swiftly, fanning herself, ignoring the curious looks as she slipped past clusters of guests toward the doors. The palm behind which she had just sinned — scandalously, foolishly — felt as though it still bore witness to her downfall.

"Isabella?" Rosalind's voice stopped her halfway to the foyer. Her sister's brow was furrowed, her expression soft with concern. "Are you unwell?"

"I think I have the beginnings of a megrim," Isabella said quickly, clutching her fan tighter to hide her trembling hands. "The noise and the heat — it has quite overwhelmed me."

Rosalind's gaze searched her face, not entirely convinced. "You look flushed."

"From the heat," Isabella said, managing a faint smile. "If you do not mind, I should like to go home."

"Of course," Rosalind said immediately. "Wait here. I shall have the carriage brought round and let Ravensmere know."

Within minutes they were inside the ducal carriage, the heavy door closing with a dull thud behind them. The sound seemed to seal Isabella into her own thoughts. The vehicle smelled faintly of lavender sachets and leather. Outside, the cobbled streets gleamed from an earlier rain, lamplight reflected in puddles that flashed by as the wheels turned. Each passing light seemed to flare across the glass, then fade, just as fleeting as her good sense had been under Whitmore's touch.

Had anyone seen them? Come morning, would she be the on-dit? Would her reputation be in ruins? Rosalind sat opposite her, studying her far too closely for her liking.

"You are certain you are not ill, my dear?"

Isabella looked out the window, her reflection faint in the glass. "Quite certain. Just a headache, I promise."

"I can send for a physician if the megrim worsens."

"That will not be necessary."

Rosalind hesitated. "Then perhaps you will tell

me what has truly happened to put you so out of sorts?"

Isabella's head snapped around. "Truly? Why would you ask me that?" Was her distress so obvious that her sister sensed more than she was saying? Rosalind was married, had been courted by a man of similar means and nature to Whitmore, perhaps she did sense more than Isabella gave her credit for.

Her sister smiled faintly. "You are not the sort to take flight from a ballroom. And your color when you left... It was not from a megrim, dearest. It was something else. Your eyes were bright, even if your skin was pink, and your lips, well, they looked a little swollen..."

Isabella sighed and pressed her gloved hands together in her lap. The fine stitching of her gown seemed suddenly suffocating. Her stays too tight. She wished she could unlace her thoughts as easily as fabric. "I am being foolish," she said at last.

"I have known you to be many things," Rosalind said, "but foolish has never been one of them. Tell me what is afoot."

Isabella looked down, her voice quiet as she prepared herself to tell her eldest sibling what conflicting thoughts and feelings she was suffering of late. "I think I may like him."

Saying the words aloud lifted a little of the weight that had settled on her. Could she trust him? Did she want to give him such power over her? What if he was merely teasing like he so liked to do? What if he was merely toying with her before someone else sashayed across his path.

Rosalind blinked. "Him?"

"Whitmore." The name left her lips like a confession. Beautiful, wicked, could kiss her off her feet and make her feel as though she were floating, Whitmore...

Her sister's eyes softened, but she said nothing for several long seconds.

"I do not think he likes me in return," Isabella added quickly, as if saying it aloud might lessen the sting. "Not truly. Not as one ought."

Rosalind tilted her head. "And what makes you so certain?"

"Because men like him do not marry women like me who want a love match," she said simply. "He could have any lady of the *ton*, any number of beauties who hang on his every word and not care if he never loved them in return." She sighed. "I'm certain he's only spending time with me — not because I am exceptional, but because I am safe. Because he knows I would never expect him to offer for me. Because I'm a little diversion to make his Season more enjoyable."

Her mind flashed back to the moment behind the palm — his hand at her waist, his mouth claiming hers as if the very air between them might burn. The press of his lips, the taste of brandy and heat made her thirst for more. For that instant, she had almost believed their friendship or whatever it was happening between them meant something. But men like Whitmore did not kiss women like her for love. They did it for sport. For curiosity. To get one into their bed.

Rosalind smiled gently. "You do not give yourself enough credit, Isabella. Whitmore is a complicated man, but that does not mean he is incapable of affection. Mayhap up until now, he's merely not found anyone who has challenged him. Has not found a woman who has told him to do as they please instead of himself."

Isabella let out a quiet laugh, unsure if any of what Rosalind said was the case. "He is incapable of sincerity, I think. Everything he says is wrapped up in charm and jest. I do not know when to believe him — or if I ever should."

Rosalind regarded her with that older-sister patience Isabella had always half-admired, half-resented. "Men," Rosalind said after a pause, "often take time to understand what is before them. Especially those accustomed to getting what they want with little effort. Sometimes it takes losing something — or nearly mislaying it — for them to realize it's worth fighting for."

Isabella's throat tightened. Did that mean she ought to wait? To give him a chance to see her differently? To see if he admitted to feeling more for her than anyone else who came before? She frowned. What if he never did any of those things? What if she wasted her heart on a man who would only laugh at her naïveté?

The gentle sway of the carriage and the steady rhythm of hooves filled the quiet. Isabella stared down at her hands, twisting the edge of her glove between her fingers. She wanted to believe Rosalind, but the memory of Whitmore's startled expression after she had asked if he meant to marry her when they were at the park replayed in her mind again and again.

He had looked stricken, panicked — as though she had pulled the ground from under his feet. That, more than anything, had hurt. Because it told her all she needed to know. He had wanted the kiss, nothing else.

He kissed you again this evening, Isabella. What if you're wrong...

"I think you give him too much credit," she said softly. "He is not a man in search of worth — only amusement."

Rosalind leaned back, clasping the seat as the carriage jostled around a corner. "And yet he kissed you, I believe, even if you have not admitted as much to me yet. But I know a kissed mouth when I see one, and your lips are certainly that."

"The kiss was not affection," Isabella said bitterly. "That was...impulse. We had argued and Whitmore thought to chastise me."

"Perhaps is it as you say, or he was so jealous he couldn't control himself, even in a ballroom surrounded by the *ton*." Rosalind met her gaze. "Often impulsive actions reveal what we are trying hardest to hide."

Isabella looked up. "You sound as though you're defending him."

"I wish for my sister to be happy." Rosalind smiling faintly. "If Whitmore has the power to do that, then I cannot condemn him too quickly."

Happy. The word felt foreign in Isabella's chest. She had not been truly content in years — not since before her first disastrous Season, when she had still believed that love came to those who waited. Now she only believed in caution. In disappointment. And yet the thought of Whitmore — his grin, his teasing eyes, the weight of his hand at her back — stirred something perilously close to hope.

"I do not wish to be a fool, Rosalind," she whispered. "To pine after a man who thinks of me as nothing more than a diversion."

"You are not a fool," Rosalind said. "You are human. We do not choose where affection settles — we decide what we do with it."

Isabella swallowed hard, her gaze dropping once more to her gloves. What was she to do with it? With this ache that made her heart throb whenever she thought of him? She wanted to banish it, to bury it deep and never let it see light again. But beneath the pain was a strange, fluttering warmth — a longing that refused to die.

"Then I shall try to do nothing with it at all," she said finally.

Rosalind clucked her tongue. "Ah, that would be wise indeed — if it were possible, but I fear you'll sadly disappoint yourself, my dear."

They rode in silence for a time, the clatter of hooves on cobblestones filling the air. Isabella tried to think of anything else — the upcoming garden party, the endless fittings for gowns, the tedious gossip of the *ton*. But every thought circled back to him.

To his voice. To his laugh. To the way he had looked at her as if no one else in the world existed. And to that moment when he had pulled away, breathless, his eyes dark with something she could not name. Desire? Confusion? Regret? It haunted her now, a question with no answer.

"I danced with Lord Lennox this evening," she said at last, breaking the silence and changing the subject.

Rosalind nodded. "And what did you think of him?"

"He is...kind," Isabella said, choosing her words carefully. "Attentive. And very proper. The sort of man every mother hopes her daughter will marry."

"Which means he bored you," Rosalind said with a light laugh.

"Not bored," Isabella said quickly. "Simply... uninspired."

Her sister grinned. "Inspiration rarely sustains a marriage, my dear. Kindness does. Stability. A man who will not bring you pain or scandal, but I recommend love and desire above all else. Everything else is merely filler."

Isabella nodded. After tonight with Whitemore, she certainly could see the sense in desiring as well as loving one's husband. "Lord Lennox seems incapable to inspire either in me at present, but I suppose that may change."

"Then I would encourage you to learn more of him if you're set against Whitmore," Rosalind said gently. "You might find that your heart has room for someone less reckless. It is not always the storm that brings happiness, Isabella — sometimes it is the calm."

The calm. Isabella let the words settle in her mind. Perhaps tranquility was what she needed — to steady herself, to remind her heart that not every thrilling thing was meant to be chased. Still, the memory of Whitmore's mouth, the heat of his breath, made that resolution waver. Could one truly crave calm when one had tasted chaos and liked it?

Isabella turned her gaze out onto Mayfair. The

carriage lanterns threw shifting reflections on the glass, and for a fleeting moment she imagined she could still see Whitmore's dark eyes staring back at her, filled with that maddening mix of arrogance and something else she dared not name.

"Perhaps," she said softly. "But I am not certain calm would suit me either."

Rosalind laughed. "Oh, I know it would not. Still, you might try it to be sure, just the same."

Isabella smiled despite herself. "I shall try."

"Good." Rosalind sat back, satisfied. "You will see him again, I imagine — Lord Lennox."

"Yes. He said as much."

"And Whitmore?"

Isabella hesitated. "He will no doubt be everywhere I am, as always. But it matters little now."

"You are certain?"

"Yes," she said firmly, though the word trembled faintly at the edges. In truth, she did not feel certain of anything. Only that she could not endure this ache much longer — the waiting, the wondering, the foolish hoping that he might look at her differently, love her as she'd want.

Love?

"I have made up my mind. Whatever I thought might be between Whitmore and me was foolishness. He has no intention of anything real, and I shall not mistake a kiss for affection or hopes for a happy future."

Rosalind reached across and touched her hand. "You are strong, Isabella. But do not close yourself off so tightly that you miss what presents itself to you. I do not wish to see you married, unsatisfied and unhappy."

"I shall try to keep my heart intact first," she said with a determination she did not feel. "Then perhaps I shall consider opening it again."

Rosalind squeezed her fingers gently. "A fair bargain I suppose."

The carriage turned down Grosvenor Square, the familiar sight of Ravensmere House coming into view. The iron gates glistened with rain, and lamplight gleamed across the windows. Inside, a fire would be waiting, warm and steady — so unlike the turmoil she carried within her chest.

As the carriage slowed, Isabella glanced once more out into the misty dark, where the lamps burned in the distance. Somewhere in that city, Whitmore would be drinking, laughing, pretending as though nothing had changed.

But for her, everything had.

She took a deep breath and squared her shoulders. She would not pine. She would not be the lovesick fool in some whispered story among the *ton*. She would go forward, as she always had — with grace, with purpose, and perhaps with someone who might truly value her.

"I shall give myself time and choose wisely, I promise, but should Lord Lennox call at our at home, please have him received."

Rosalind smiled approvingly. "Of course, whatever you wish."

The carriage rolled to a halt and a footman opened the door, cool night air rushing in.

As Isabella stepped down, she looked up at the sky. The clouds were parting, revealing the faint glimmer of starlight. For a moment she let herself believe that perhaps the kiss — that dangerous, unforgettable kiss — could be the beginning of something, not the end.

The memory of his mouth ghosted over hers, and she knew the truth. No amount of time would make her forget the taste of Whitmore's kiss. Not even if she pretended it were so.

CHAPTER

EIGHTEEN

Whitmore woke to a blade behind his eyes and the miserable certainty that sleep had done nothing to improve his disposition. The clock on the mantel said half past one. Trust him to greet the afternoon like a rake who had earned his reputation, and feel none the better for it.

He dragged himself into his study, sleeves rolled, cravat in one fist, and stared at the untouched pile of invitations and tradesmen's bills as if they had offended him personally. They probably had. The room smelled of yesterday's fire, beeswax, and a faint echo of brandy that turned his stomach. He poured water, drank, poured another, and told himself he would think of ledgers and tenant repairs and anything sensible.

He thought of her instead.

Lady Isabella Ravensmere. The shape of her name in his head was a problem all of its own.

He had kissed her in the park, argued with her at a ball, and then kissed her again behind a palm where anyone with a taste for scandal might have found them. There was no chance he would take any money from the duke. What may have started as a wager, was long past that now. In his sleep, he dreamed of her mouth. When he woke, drenched in sweat and hard as stone, he forced himself to be practical.

Practicality lasted as long as it took his butler to inform him that the Duchess of Ravensmere was hosting an at-home this afternoon, and a number of callers already seen approaching the house on Grosvenor Square were many indeed.

The phrase a number of callers tightened something unpleasant in his chest. "Which callers?" Whitmore asked, striving for indifference and failing to find it.

"I could not say, my lord," the butler replied. "Only that there were several gentlemen, or so a footman informed me on his way back from errands. It seems quite the place to be."

Perfect. A parade of well-appointed men with tidy intentions and dull souls. He yanked on his coat, forgot his cravat, remembered it, tied it badly, and strode for the door.

"Your horse, my lord?" the butler called after him.

"Later." He was already on the steps, hailing the first passing hackney like a man pursued. He was not pursued, unless one counted good sense, which he had successfully outrun since he first saw Isabella smile.

The hackney smelled of damp wool and old tobacco. Whitmore sat forward, knees braced, while the city streamed by in jolts and clatters. He told himself he was only going to pay a polite call on

Ravensmere. One ought to visit a friend when one had the time. He told himself he was curious to see which gentlemen believed themselves worthy of Isabella. He told himself many things.

None of them eased the repugnant jealousy that ran hot in his veins.

The Ravensmere townhouse was already busy. A steady trickle of callers ascended the steps with bouquets and hopeful faces. Whitmore paid the jarvey and took the stairs two at a time, ignoring the look of surprise the footman gave him at his eagerness.

And in all truth he could not blame the fellow. He had lost all common sense.

The at-home was arranged with the duchess's customary elegance, flowers in tasteful profusion, the air warm with tea and conversation. Lady visitors clustered near the windows, gentlemen stood at strategic angles of approach, and there, upon a small sofa set slightly apart as if by invisible design, sat Bells. Rosalind was near enough to chaperone, far enough to allow conversation. The balance would have made a general proud.

He took in a deep breath and drank in the sight of her. Isabella looked like serenity and perfection. Her gown of pale green softened her eyes and made her skin glow. She laughed at something Lord Lennox said, and Whitmore felt the peculiar sensation of his stomach and his temper flexing.

There were not one or two callers. There were five. He recognized most of them. Young, well mannered, tidy fortunes. Good families, few vices, and a terrifying ability to talk earnestly about the weather. Lord Lennox, the traveler, stood closest to

Isabella's seat, the fellow's posture relaxed, his smile easy. A decent man. The sort of decent that got a woman safely married.

The sort of decent Whitmore was certainly not.

He made his bow to the duchess first like a gentleman, received her welcome, perceived the faint tightening at the edges of her smile that suggested she suspected him of something and had not decided what, then turned to Isabella and Lord Lennox.

"Lady Isabella," he said.

"Lord Whitmore," she returned. Her voice was calm. Her gaze was not. There was a spark there that met his, clashed with it, and set the ground between them alight.

"Whitmore." Lord Lennox offered his hand. "A pleasure."

"Likewise," Whitmore said. He took the man's measure in the shake. Firm. Honest. Blast him.

"You were not at White's last evening?" Lord Lennox stated, conversationally. "I heard your steward kept you until ungodly hours."

"He has a talent for it," Whitmore said. "He keeps a list of matters to vex me and checks them off one by one." He turned to Isabella. "I trust you are well after the ball."

"Well enough," she said.

He waited for her to color. She did not. She only looked at him as if daring him to try something ill advised. He had never needed so little encouragement.

Lord Lennox resumed his talking points, affable as a summer breeze. "Her Grace's at-home is quite the scene this afternoon. I had not planned to add to your crowded parlor, Your Grace," he called toward the duchess with a smile, "but it seems half the beau monde took the same notion."

"It is kind of you to come," the duchess answered. "Isabella enjoys good conversation."

"Conversation," Whitmore said, "is a fine art."

"Indeed," Lord Lennox agreed. "I was telling Lady Isabella about Florence. The galleries are beyond compare."

"The galleries," Whitmore said. "Yes. Crowded, are they not?"

"Inspiring," Lord Lennox corrected. "There is a chapel where the light itself seems to sing."

"Does it, by God, how extraordinary," Whitmore said, and received a look from the duchess that reminded him he was in a drawing room, not his club.

Isabella's mouth quirked, before she quickly hid it behind her teacup. She did not, however, send him away. That felt like a victory in itself, however petty he may be acting right at this moment.

Lord Lennox continued, undisturbed and too stupid to know that Whitmore had been mocking him. "I had hoped to return this autumn, yet London has its charms."

"So it does," Whitmore replied, allowing himself the smallest glance at Isabella that said quite clearly which charm he meant. She ignored him. Or pretended to. Her fingers tightened on her saucer.

"Tell us, Whitmore," Lord Lennox said, "have you any plans for travel this Season?"

"None," Whitmore said. "I find my interests are, at present, closer to home."

The duchess coughed behind her glove. Isabella

set down her cup with a gentle click that felt like a warning bell.

Lord Lennox smiled. “Then perhaps you will join a party to Richmond tomorrow next. Lady Isabella mentioned she enjoys the outdoors and there is a sweet brook that runs through the grounds. A day out riding in such a picturesque landscape sounds just the thing, does it not?”

“It does indeed.” Whitmore would have left it at that if his better sense had not fled his person entirely. “Particularly when the company suits.”

“Company tells for much,” Lord Lennox agreed. “Lady Isabella has such grace that any company is improved by her presence.”

Whitmore almost liked him less for being sincere.

He took a chair he had not been offered and applied himself to getting in the way. It was a talent. He inquired after Lord Lennox’s opinion of horseflesh, then dismissed it kindly, which made the man laugh, even if it were at his own expense. He steered the topic to books, then disagreed on three authors in succession, all while smiling as if he were enjoying himself. He complimented Isabella’s gown, then complimented the duchess’s taste, then turned back to Lord Lennox to ask if Italy had taught him anything useful, since the gentleman seemed quite oblivious to the fact that he seemed to gloat over his travels.

“Patience,” Lord Lennox said, amused. “Enough to know when to yield a conversation and when not to.”

“A useful skill,” Whitmore said. “I have not learned it.”

"So I see..."

Isabella set down her cup again. "Then perhaps you might practice on someone less inclined to notice."

"And miss the pleasure of your notice? Never," Whitmore said.

"You're impossible."

"So I have heard."

Lord Lennox cleared his throat, and Isabella met his lordship's gaze. "Lord Lennox," Isabella said sweetly, turning away from Whitmore, "you were telling me about the chapel. The light that sings."

"I was," Lord Lennox said. He described it with the simple pleasure of a man who loved what he had seen. Isabella listened with real attention, asking small questions. Whitmore watched their exchange with something sharp in his throat. It was not only jealousy. It was the recognition that Lord Lennox did not perform. He simply spoke. He made Isabella comfortable. He did not crowd her or bait her or try to read her thoughts like a page he was certain he owned.

Whitmore changed tack. Humor had always been his shield. He used it now and hated himself for it. "Did Florence improve your dancing as well?" he asked. "I understand the Italians move with notable elegance."

"I could not say." Lord Lennox smiled. "Lady Isabella might judge. She suffered my waltz and was too kind to fault it."

"Her kindness is a trap." Whitmore met her startled gaze and wished they were alone. Away from this pompous fool who said pretty things in her ears. He wanted her alone, to himself. He did not like to share, and he certainly would not like to share her. "She lures a man into contentment, then slays him with honesty."

Isabella arched a brow. "If I slay you, my lord, it will not be with honesty."

"Ah," he said softly. "Then I am safe."

"You are never safe where I am concerned." Their eyes caught, held. It was a foolish thing to do in a room full of people. They did it anyway.

Lord Lennox set his teacup down with a clatter. "I believe I spy a rather handsome cake. With your permission, Lady Isabella, I shall fetch a slice, unless you would like one brought over for a light repast."

"Thank you, my lord," she said. "I am quite content."

"Contentment is a temporary state," Whitmore murmured, and earned himself a glance that could have cut wire.

Lord Lennox smiled, offered a nod, and rose. He crossed to the table with the calm of a man who recognized a battlefield and chose to fetch cake rather than die upon it.

Whitmore did not notice he had gone until Isabella turned and scolded him beneath her breath. "You have made him leave me."

"Cake called to him," Whitmore said.

"You chased him with your talk and your temper. If he does not return, I shall blame you."

"I welcome your blame."

"You are unbearable."

"And yet, here I sit."

"Only because I cannot very well push you to

the floor," she hissed, and smiled at a passing matron as if she had said something sweet.

He stood abruptly. Movement might save him from saying worse. "I will go and plague Ravensmere in the library."

"You will do no such thing," she said, rising too. "My brother-in-law is at his club."

"Then I shall plague his books. He has a well-stocked library. I shall be content to wait."

"You will not." She took one step after him, then another, then kept going without seeming to think she did so. They drifted together from the parlor, through the soft net of people and talk, and no one took much notice. A lady crossing to examine the piano forte, a gentleman admiring a portrait. They moved into the passage beyond, then into Ravensmere's library. It was quiet there, the air cooler, the light softened by late afternoon.

"Now," she said, voice low. "You have done your worst. Lord Lennox is fetching cake to avoid throttling you, and I am cross. What precisely did you hope to accomplish here today?"

"I had planned nothing," he admitted. "I am not thinking clearly."

"On that point we agree."

"Excellent." He slipped his hands into his coat pockets, certain that if he did not, they would occupy themselves with something unspeakable. Like pulling her against him. Kissing her again and relishing in her surrender. "We are of one mind."

"We are of no such thing." She came closer, and he could see the faint flush at her throat, the quick rise and fall of her breath. "You are jealous, and you need to leave. Stop playing with me as if I'm nothing but a game."

"I am not." Her words struck him like a slap. That he had started to believe them as true also did not help his annoyance.

"You are." Her voice softened. "And you are trying to make it difficult for me to find a husband."

"I am certainly not."

"You are. You do it without thinking because you cannot help yourself."

"That is absurd." But was it? Even he could see that was exactly what he was doing. But to what end? He wasn't even sure if he wished to marry Isabella. He glanced down at her, and something softened in his chest.

"Is it?" she said. "Then explain why you arrived here without an invitation and inserted yourself like a stray alley cat among my callers."

"Stray alley cats are charming."

"They mark their territory everywhere."

"I might too."

"I would expect no less," she said, and that unbalanced him entirely.

He took a step back, found the wall at his shoulders, and wondered when she had become so eloquent at putting him off-kilter. Jealousy tasted like salt in his mouth. It was ridiculous. She was free to court and be courted. He had known it would happen. He had told himself he wanted it to happen. He had not expected the sensation that accompanied the sight of her laughing with another man—which felt very much like falling from a horse and not caring if he hit the ground—to be an outcome he'd suffer.

"You should not marry him." The words wrong, but he was unable not to voice them.

She stared at him, clearly confounded. "You do not get to say such a thing to me."

"I know."

"You do not get to decide who is worthy."

"I know."

"You do not wish to marry me yourself, and yet you cannot bear that someone else might."

He shut his eyes. "That is not fair."

"It is precisely fair. You do not know what you want, and in the meantime you ruin my chances of finding what may make me happy."

"And he will make you happy?" he scoffed. "What do you want, Bells? Really?" His voice was rough and he felt like everything hinged on what she said. "You kiss me and then allow Lord Lennox to court you?"

"I want to be chosen," she said simply. "For myself, and not because someone feels sorry for me, or they're desperate to marry an heiress. Or because someone sees a pitiful spinster who's in need of saving, giving them a taste of what they have never had." She paused. "If Lord Lennox proves himself a good man, I will not let your interest in me of the carnal kind to frighten him away. You may desire me, but you do not love me and that is why you must stop."

He took a fortifying breath. "I do not mean to frighten him away. I like Lennox."

"You cannot possibly like him after how you just acted."

"I do," he said miserably, hating that everything she said was true. He was a bastard, kissing her, wanting her in his bed, and all the while, pretending it would not affect her. That she enjoyed the game as much as he. Of course she wanted a love match, something he could not give.

She blinked, and something in her expression gentled. "Then leave me to my callers, Whitmore."

He reached for her, needing to touch her, to have her in his grasp. "Tell me you will not marry him without being truly certain he is everything that will make you happy," he said before he could stop himself, closing the space separating them. "Tell me that if our kisses taught you anything, it is that you deserve passion and love, not just a suitable, convenient marriage."

They were close now. The room seemed very small, the air crackling with unsaid words and silent promises. He could smell roses and the soft perfume of her skin and soap. "Bells," he pleaded.

"Do not," she warned, trying to move away and coming up against a bookcase at her back.

"One last kiss," he asked.

"No." Her answer was determined, but her eyes danced with longing, burned with need.

"I cannot seem to do as you say. I'm sorry." He moved. Or she did. Perhaps they both did. One moment they stood divided by a breath, and the next his arms gathered her in, drawing her close. He kissed her, deep and long, and she melted into his body, suspiciously made for him.

She gasped, the soft, needy sound undoing the knot of his self-control. His mouth slanted, found hers and relished her surrender. He gentled and deepened, scolded and apologized without words. He picked her up and set her on the ledge of the bookshelf, clasped her face and felt the flutter of her pulse beneath his fingers, the answering throb of his own, and knew he was lost.

He broke away, breathing hard, resting his forehead against hers. "I am a fool."

"Yes," she said, breathless, eyes bright with anger and something else. "And you are cruel."

"I do not mean to be."

"Then stop."

"I do not know how."

She closed her eyes for a moment, as if assembling patience. "Go, Whitmore. Before someone finds us. Before you do something neither of us can mend or change the outcome of."

He stepped back at once. That, at least, he could do right. He looked at her, memorized the set of her mouth and the quiver of her lashes and the proud line of her chin. She moved to stand and he fled like a man whose skin had grown too small to contain him, shameful and without honor.

He made it as far as the front steps before he remembered he had not brought his horse. A footman hailed a hackney for him with the serene judgment only a faultless servant could convey.

Inside the jolting carriage, Whitmore pressed his fists to his knees and stared at nothing. His heart would not steady. He could still taste her. He could still hear her saying *I want to be chosen*, and the words had settled in his bones where he could not dislodge them.

He did not want her for himself. Of course he did not. He was not ready. He was ill suited. He was, by all accounts, unreliable. He could list a dozen reasons. They sounded increasingly like excuses spoken by a man who feared the one thing he had never allowed himself, which was to want something that might break him if he could not have it.

He let his head fall back against the worn squabs and laughed once, low and without humor.

He was not certain what, precisely, he had found himself in. A courtship. A calamity. A story that refused to go the way he had written it.

He only knew that he had left her with the taste of his apology on her lips, and every instinct he possessed screamed at him to turn around and do the one thing that might make this worse, which was to ask her what she wanted and offer it like a vow.

Instead, he told the jarvey to drive on, and the city swallowed him up, including his honor.

CHAPTER NINETEEN

The following evening the ducal carriage slowed before the Fairborne townhouse, the outside lamps spilling warm golden light across the cobblestone streets. Music drifted faintly through the open windows, the hum of violins and soft laughter slipping into the night.

Isabella drew a steadying breath. She had nearly refused the invitation. Lady Mariah Fairborne had been a friend during their first Season—a sweet, eager debutante with a tendency to speak before she thought. She was now married, and Isabella had not yet attended any of her old friend's small gatherings—feeling a little out of place with most in attendance who were married and settled. Still, it was something to do, and staying home with her thoughts was dangerous.

Thoughts that swirled in a constant circle regarding one particular marquess.

She glanced at her maid seated across from her. "Are you certain you do not mind waiting downstairs for me? I'm certain Mariah's servants will be nice."

"Yes, my lady," Mary said, folding her hands primly. "I know Lady Fairborne's lady's maid, and it'll be nice to see her again."

Isabella smiled, relieved to hear this. "Very well. It should not be a late evening."

She hoped...

In truth, she had no true idea how long the rout would go for. The last twenty-four hours since Whitmore had fled her house had been hours of confusion, of words unspoken, and emotions she had no wish to name. Perhaps the music and good conversation, card games and music would still her thoughts. Perhaps she would, for a few hours, forget the way Lord Whitmore's kiss had lingered like a ghost upon her lips.

The footman opened the carriage door, and she stepped down into the night. A soft drizzle had begun to fall, dotting the stones and lending a faint sheen to the street. She adjusted her shawl and ascended the steps, her pulse quickening as she heard the muffled sound of guests within.

Inside, the warmth enveloped her. Mariah's townhouse was not large, but it had been arranged with care. The drawing room glittered with candles and gilt mirrors, filled with the rustle of silk gowns and the murmur of polite laughter. The scent of beeswax and glass-house flowers mingled with the faint powder of perfumes.

"Lady Isabella!" Mariah hurried forward, her blue skirts swaying, her expression one of genuine delight. "I did not think you'd come. You're always so elusive."

"Not elusive, merely dull," Isabella said with a

small smile, bussing her friend's cheeks with a small kiss.

"Nonsense." Mariah took her hands. "You bring refinement wherever you go. Come—there are a few familiar faces, and I have arranged some entertainment for later. A musical evening, nothing too grand. We are all so weary of dancing, are we not?"

"Indeed."

She allowed herself to be led farther in. The company was modest, perhaps thirty guests, seated in conversational groups. No card tables. No dancing yet—though there was ample room should they decide to do so later. The atmosphere was easy, comfortable, the kind that lulled one into forgetting the rules of the *ton* for an hour or two.

Isabella accepted a glass of wine from a footman and found a seat near the edge of the room. From there, she could watch the guests without being drawn into serious conversation. Her gaze lingered on the piano forte, her mind dangerously slipping to what happened yesterday. She shook the wayward thoughts aside, determined not to think of Whitmore tonight.

She took a slow sip of her wine.

It had been a day since she'd seen he whom she should not name. Since the third shockingly good kiss. One that had made her want to wrap her legs about his waist and force him to stay. To have him continue the sweet, delectable seduction.

She had expected to feel relief after he left—anger, perhaps, at him kissing her so shamelessly yet again. Instead, she felt unmoored. Her mind replayed every look, every word, every glide of his tongue, his warm breath, his eyes that burned with fire. A fire that lit the one muffled within her.

The way he had pressed her against the bookshelf as if she were the only woman in the world he desired, then fled as though she were a plague he must escape.

It was for the best, she told herself. He did not wish to marry her. He had said as much in his own way. Better to accept his aversion and move on.

But her body did not quite believe what her mind insisted upon.

Damn the man.

An impromptu performance from Sir Alcott began. A gentleman reciting a sonnet about love's endurance. His voice was trembling, his delivery far too earnest, and yet the words cut through her more keenly than she wished to admit.

Love that conquers all. Love that survives silence and pride.

She stared into her glass, feeling the room close around her. She had conquered nothing.

"Lady Isabella Ravensmere," Mariah murmured near her side. "May I present Sir Alcott?"

She looked up to find a tanned, tall gentleman bowing before her. He was handsome in the clean, well-ordered way that society admired. Fair hair, clear eyes, not a wrinkle in his cravat. She smiled and inclined her head as he took the seat beside her.

"Lady Fairborne speaks highly of you," he said. "She told me you were quite the musician when inclined."

"I used to play, yes."

"Will you again tonight?"

"I think not."

He chuckled softly. "I suppose that is fortunate for the rest of us, then. We may enjoy without comparison."

The comment was kind, and she returned his smile. He was perfectly polite, perfectly interested, and perfectly uninteresting. But polite conversation was safer than brooding, quick-witted remarks that sometimes cut. She let him speak, nodding as he told her of his estate, his sister's marriage, and his fondness for horses.

She did not expect the sudden hush that swept the room. The soft rustle of fans stilled. Some ladies in her sight turned their heads and without hesitation Isabella followed their gaze toward the doorway.

She felt the blood drain from her face.

Whitmore stood there, freshly arrived, gloves in hand.

Her heart stumbled.

He was not supposed to be here. This was a quiet evening, a small gathering among old friends. Why had he come?

He caught sight of her at once. Of course he did. His gaze swept the room, cool and assessing, until it landed on her—and held.

The air thickened. She felt every breath between them. Then he moved through the room, bowing to Mariah, exchanging a few polite words, before approaching where she sat.

"Lady Isabella," he said evenly, though she saw the faint curl of mischief in his mouth. "How pleasant to see you here."

"Lord Whitmore." Her tone was as composed as

she could manage, but she couldn't help but feel he was up to something, and if not, soon would be. "I did not expect you to be in attendance."

"Nor I, but Lord Pye over by the mantel is a good friend and wished for me to attend. I was under the impression this was to be an evening of poetry. I came prepared to be bored, but alas, the night has improved."

"Then you're easily entertained."

His eyes glinted. "Is that a challenge?"

Sir Alcott cleared his throat beside her. "I was just telling Lady Isabella about my stables, Whitmore. Perhaps you've heard of my new mare—"

"I have," Whitmore interrupted smoothly. "A fine creature. Though not as fine as the one Lady Isabella rides. I've never seen a horse obey so gracefully."

"Perhaps it is the rider," Alcott said with an amiable smile.

"Perhaps," Whitmore replied, a small smile playing on his wicked mouth, his attention solely on her. She stared at his mouth, one she'd not stopped thinking about. She ground her teeth, wishing him anywhere but here.

"You gentlemen will frighten the poor creature with all your praise."

"Do you speak of the horse or yourself?" Whitmore murmured.

"Whichever you prefer." She forced a tight smile, wanting the subject to change.

Sir Alcott laughed, seemingly oblivious to the undercurrent. How that was so, Isabella could not fathom.

"Ah, Mariah mentioned there may be a duet

this evening," Isabella said, watching a couple of guests seat themselves at the instrument, happy a diversion had presented itself. "This will be most entertaining."

"If you say so," Whitmore quipped, moving to stand beside her.

The pianists began, a lilting tune, gentle and romantic. Isabella fought not to be distracted, even though she could feel Whitmore watching her as she concentrated on the pianists.

She attempted to ignore him, to focus on the music, but his presence pressed against her like a physical caress. The melody rose and fell, tender and aching. Her chest tightened. It was ridiculous —mere notes, nothing more—and yet the echo of that kiss, the taste of whisky and sin, the heat of his hand against her jaw, his masculine, overwhelming body against her flesh.

Dear Lord she was a wanton.

She turned to Sir Alcott. "Will you excuse me? I need a moment, thank you."

"Of course," he said, rising at once and not questioning her absence. "I shall be here when you return."

"How kind, thank you."

She did not speak to Whitmore, merely moved toward the door and where she believed the retiring room was located. She quickened her steps, needing solitude and a moment to breathe. The house was smaller than most grand townhouses, the corridors narrow, the walls close. She found a door at the end of the corridor and slipped inside, hoping for solitude.

The faint scent of cigar smoke and beeswax

polish met her senses, and the muted green of the billiard table caught what little light filtered through the curtained windows. Not the retiring room, but good enough. Cues rested neatly in their rack. The hush of the room enclosed around her like a balm and was just what she needed.

She drew a deep breath, pressing a hand to her chest. Foolish. Entirely reckless.

The sound of footsteps in the hall made her shoulders stiffen a moment before the door opened.

"Running away again?"

The deep timbre of his voice evoked emotions in her she wanted to ignore, to pretend didn't make her ache. She turned. He had followed her. "Must you always intrude?"

"It's my forte."

"It is a flaw."

"Possibly both."

She drew a breath, steadying her tone. "Why are you here? Why must you be everywhere I am?"

"I could ask you the same."

"This was not your affair to attend. Mariah is my friend. You should have denied your friend the pleasure of your company if you knew I was going to be here."

He frowned, coming into the room and shutting the door. She didn't like that they were alone, several doors from the safety of the rout.

"But that would have disappointed Lord Pye and I do not like disappointing my friends."

She laughed once, brittle and full of mocking. "You expect me to believe that?"

"I did not know you would be here, that was entirely by chance."

"You should leave." She wanted him gone, far, far away from her where she wouldn't be tempted by the very sight of his handsome face. She wanted to stomp her foot, pretend that he wasn't niggling and wigging under her skin, imbedding himself there like a barb.

He stepped closer, his voice softening. "Do you truly wish that?"

She should. God help her, she should. But his nearness unsettled her, as it always did, and she could not voice her request again for him to leave. The memory of his last kiss haunted her every breath, replaying in her mind like a forbidden melody.

"You confuse me, Whitmore," she admitted quietly. "You say one thing and do another. You tell me you are not ready to marry, and yet you act as though—"

"As though what?"

"As though I belong to you."

The words hung between them. His jaw tightened, and she saw something flicker in his eyes—guilt, desire, fear.

"I do not know what I want," he disclosed. "Only that when I see you with another man, I want to break something."

Her heart stuttered. "Then you are covetous. Are you finally admitting to it?"

"Undeniably."

"And yet you will not marry me."

He gave a short laugh, harsh and self-mocking. "You make it sound so simple."

"It is simple." Her voice trembled. "You either wish to court me, or you do not." She swallowed when he moved another step nearer. The faint scent of sandalwood clung to him, and it was an aroma she'd always relished.

Damn the man.

"I fear I will only ever disappoint you, Bells."

His response was not what she wished or expected to hear. Her temper spiked and she narrowed her eyes. "Then why are you here?"

"Because I could not stay away."

Her breath caught. For a long moment, neither spoke. The muffled music from the drawing room drifted faintly through the closed door. The air between them hummed with an unseen blaze.

He reached for her hand, hesitating only an instant before his fingers linked with hers. The touch was reverent and sent a tremor through her body.

"This is wrong," she whispered.

"Everything about us feels flawed," he said. "And yet I cannot stay away."

She knew she should step back, end this madness. Instead, she met his gaze, saw the raw confusion there—the same bewilderment that lived in her own heart—and all sensible thought vanished.

He reached for her, but she was already moving toward him. Their lips met, held.

The kiss was not gentle, but then, when was it when it came to them? The caress was urgent, hungry, a collision of two people who knew they ought to stop and could not. His hand slid to her waist, drawing her against him, and the world narrowed to the sound of their breaths and the soft patter of rain against the windows.

He picked her up and set her on the billiards table as if she were as light as a feather. He pressed against her, and she slipped her leg about his waist, pulling him close. He rolled his hips against her core, and she gasped at the sweet ache that thrummed there.

"Whitmore..." she groaned.

"Hartley... No titles." His strong, large hand encased her ankle, slipping along her silk stocking, leaving goosebumps in the wake of his touch. Her breath caught as his caress did not cease but continued to her thigh. He squeezed her flesh, and she shuddered. She gathered her gown gathered at her waist, opening herself to him, leaving no discretion between them.

"So damn beautiful. You make me want to be a different man."

His words left her voiceless. He kissed her again and she gasped when his fingers slipped over her mons and caressed her aching flesh. "Yes, Hartley."

He groaned. "I love the sound of my name on your lips." His mouth took hers again, hungry and demanding. He touched her where she ached most, rolling his fingers against a place of her that she'd never thought much of before this night.

It was wonderful, maddening all in one moment. "Don't stop, whatever this madness is that you're doing." She closed her eyes and relished in the hungry kiss he bestowed against her neck.

"I have no intention of stopping," he murmured in her ear.

She bit her lip to stop herself from calling out. They were at a rout, an entertainment where they could be caught at any moment, still it wasn't enough to persuade her to stop. She doubted anything would make her ask him to pause his wicked, wonderful actions.

His hand moved, and she felt the pressure of his fingers at her core. She clutched at him, needing him close, wanting him with a desperation she'd never felt before. It was wonderful, maddening, and unlike anything she'd imagined. Was this what made her sisters have those secretive smiles, and knowing glances with their husbands?

He pressed into her, and she gasped.

"I'm imagining myself in you right now, Bells. My hand will have to do for now."

For now? Did he intend to engage in this madness again?

He kissed her again, stroking her, teasing and taking her with his hand. Her body felt as though it were having an out-of-body experience, it ached and craved with a wild immorality. She pressed against him, seeking more, wanting more.

"You sing at my touch."

His words were wicked. She nodded, breathless and perhaps senseless as well. "I do," she admitted, close to a pinnacle she wanted to tumble over, relish at the hands of a man who drove her mad.

He did not stop. Instead, he played her with an ability that left her mindless. He took her lips as pleasure unknown to her tumbled through her, contracting about her body and leaving her clutching him, needing to anchor herself lest she float off into the universe.

Only when she had regained her wits did he step back, settling her gown over her trembling legs. He raised his hand and slipped two fingers into his mouth, watching her intently as he sucked his fingers clean, his gaze burning with a need she now understood.

"You taste delicious."

She gaped, unable to form words at the sight of him and what he was doing. Dear God, she would not survive this man.

His wicked grin told her he knew he'd shocked her and was enjoying it. "We should return," he said.

She pressed a trembling hand to his chest, pushing him away with what little strength she had left. "You go. I shall return momentarily."

He stepped back at once, jaw tight, eyes dark. He bowed—an oddly formal gesture in such a moment—then turned and left her standing alone.

When she finally returned to the drawing room, her composure had been sewn back together with sheer will. Sir Alcott was still there, chatting easily with Mariah, but there was no sign of Whitmore. Had he left? The knowledge left a hollowness in her chest.

Isabella rallied herself to mingle, to laugh and pretend nothing had happened that had changed her life forever.

But in her heart, she knew that something had altered irrevocably—that every time she closed her eyes, she would remember the taste of what she could have with Whitmore if only he would relent.

And give in to what was clearly happening between them.

CHAPTER TWENTY

Whitmore woke early the following day, the pale morning light slipping through a crack in the curtains and cutting across his bed. His head pounded, though unfortunately not from drink. His body felt leaden, as if sleep had failed to wash the night from him. He dragged a hand down his face and sat up slowly, the linen sheets tangled around his legs. The faint scent of rain still clung to the room, or perhaps that was only his imagination.

He closed his eyes and sighed, still tasting her on his lips. He cursed under his breath, swung his feet to the Aubusson rug, and sat there for a long moment with his elbows on his knees. The fire had burned low. A tray sat untouched near the hearth, coffee cooling beside his breakfast his valet must have brought. He moved over to where his breakfast sat and took up the beverage and swallowed, grimacing at the cool bitterness.

The night before replayed in his mind whether he wished it or not. Isabella Ravensmere, sitting on the billiard table, the lamplight glinting off her hair, her breath quick and shallow as she gave herself to him and then promptly told him to leave. Her lips —soft, angry, willing. He had kissed her like a man possessed. Like one determined to prove he felt nothing, that he could indulge with her without consequences, and in doing so had proven he was an idiot.

"You're in love with her," he muttered. The words sounded absurd in the stillness. Love was not a thing for men like him. Desire, yes. Infatuation, often. But love required an honesty he had long forgotten how to wield.

He crossed to the window, pushing aside the curtain. Outside, the street bustled with midday noise—vendors shouting, wheels clattering, the faint clip of hooves over wet cobblestone. London was awake, indifferent to his turmoil. Somewhere out there, Isabella would be as well. Perhaps she sat with her sister over tea, discussing the next ball, or the day at Richmond that was happening today, laughing over something her sisters had done. He wondered if she laughed easily this morning, or if she too carried the ache that had settled behind his ribs.

He turned away sharply, dragging on his shirt and coat, hoisting his breeches on without care. He could not sit here stewing in memory like some moonstruck fool. Movement might dull the thoughts clawing through him. By the time he descended the stairs, the butler had opened his mouth to ask whether the carriage should be readied. "No," Whitmore said quickly, pulling on his gloves. "I'm going for a walk."

The air outside was sharp enough to clear his

head, though it did nothing to ease the restless energy coursing through him. He cut across Mayfair, boots splashing through shallow puddles. Where the hell had summer gone? Every street corner reminded him of her—Bond Street, where he had once seen her buying ribbons with her sister. Hyde Park, where she rode often with her infernally perfect mare he'd like for his own stables. He should have gone there now, if only to assure himself she was well, that she would still speak to him after hightailing it out of the rout they attended last night without so much as a goodbye.

But what right did he have to do so? She ought to be mad at him, disappointed. He certainly was.

Hartley strode along Curzon Street without direction, the damp air chilling his skin. He should have gone home, but the restless energy in his chest refused to quiet. Every step only sharpened the unease gnawing at him—something between guilt, longing, and irritation that she occupied so much of his mind.

By the time he reached his townhouse again, he had walked near two miles and felt no more settled than before. The butler met him in the hall, eyebrows raised.

"My lord, a note has arrived from the Duke of Ravensmere. The servants await your response."

He tore the seal open, scanning the neat handwriting. He and the duchess were inquiring if he was attending the outing to Richmond today. There would be picnicking, a stroll by the brook, polite laughter, and conversation he could not abide. Yet the thought of Isabella among the company tightened something deep within his chest. He told himself he might attend simply to prove he could behave with sense. To prove that last night had meant nothing.

That she meant nothing.

He tossed the note onto a table. "Tell them I'll join the party."

An hour later his horse was brought round, the glossy bay stamping impatiently on the cobbles. Whitmore swung into the saddle, the familiar leather creak grounding him. He needed the wind in his face, the distance from London's confining streets.

The party assembled near Hyde Park Gate—carriages gleaming, servants bustling, ladies bright as spring flowers despite the dull sky. He spotted Ravensmere's distinctive coach at once. The duke and duchess stood beside it, exchanging greetings with friends. Isabella was nowhere to be seen—until she stepped down from another carriage with a grace that made his breath catch in his throat.

She wore a gown of pale yellow trimmed with blue ribbons, the color of sunlight. Annoyance took hold as she came to stand beside Lord Lennox, tall and insufferably polished, offering his arm as though she belonged there.

Whitmore's fingers tightened around his reins.

He reminded himself she could do as she pleased. She owed him nothing. But as she laughed—softly, politely—at something Lennox said, Whitmore felt an unreasonable surge of dislike for the man's entire existence.

"Whitmore," Ravensmere greeted him with a knowing smile. "You look half in the mood for trouble. Good of you to join us. We ride to Richmond at once."

"Of course. I would not miss it," he said, forcing civility. He bowed to the duchess, whose perceptive eyes missed little, then turned to find Isabella already stepping into an open-air carriage—Lord Lennox at her side.

The journey began pleasantly enough. The morning mist lifted as they left the city to reveal a stretch of green countryside, dotted with grazing cattle and the occasional cottage roof glinting in the light. The party was in high spirits. Laughter drifted from the carriages, ribbons fluttered in the breeze. Whitmore tried to tell himself he was being ridiculous, that her enjoyment was a good thing.

It lasted until the road curved near a slope thick with brambles. A sudden crack split the air—wood, unmistakably—and the lead carriage lurched.

"Hold!" someone shouted. Horses whinnied in alarm.

Whitmore's stomach heaved with dread and his instincts kicked in before thought. He spurred forward his horse as the wheel splintered, and the carriage listed sharply to the side. A woman screamed. The vehicle pitched into the ditch with a sickening thud.

He was off his horse and at the wreck before the commotion settled. Ravensmere's coachman joined him, pale and shouting orders for more assistance. Whitmore ignored him, wrenching the carriage door open and reaching inside.

"Isabella!"

Her name tore from him without permission. Inside, confusion reigned—gowns tangled, hat feathers crushed, one footman trying to calm the panicked horses. Lord Lennox coughed, dazed, rubbing his temple.

But Isabella—

She sat half-sprawled on the opposite seat, eyes wide, one glove torn, a faint line of blood along her temple where she must have struck the frame.

Whitmore climbed in, his heart pounding. "Are you hurt?"

She blinked at him, stunned. "I—no, I do not think so."

He touched her chin lightly, tilting her face toward the light. The sight of that small wound sent a rush of heat through his chest that had nothing to do with anger. He wanted to throttle the coachman, the maker of the wheel, the entire blasted countryside for placing a rut on the road. Anything to undo that mark.

"You've injured yourself," he muttered. "Stay still." He pulled a handkerchief from his pocket, dabbing gently at the blood. His hand trembled.

"Whitmore, really," she said softly, attempting to smile. "It is only a scratch."

He didn't answer. The sound of her voice undid him. He'd thought he could bear seeing her with another man, but this—the sight of her pale and shaken, wounded—was intolerable.

The duchess appeared at the door. "Oh, my dearest, is everyone well? Please tell me you're unhurt?"

"Yes," Isabella called, steady now. "All is well."

Whitmore lingered a moment longer, unable to move. Her eyes—clear, green, and still a little unfocused—found his. Something passed between them, silent and heavy as the air after a storm.

"Come," he said finally, his voice rough. "You should get out. The carriage is at an angle."

He reached for her hand before he realized what he was doing. Her fingers slipped into his, small and cold. He guided her out, steadying her as she descended the broken step. When her foot wobbled, he caught her around the waist without thinking and slipped her into his arms.

The scent of her hair—roses, always roses—hit him squarely in the chest. He didn't breathe for a moment, terrified she might see everything he felt written across his face. That he loved her. That he didn't know what to do with that realization, but knew it would change him forever whatever his choice was going forward.

Lord Lennox appeared from the vehicle, adjusting his coat as if he'd suffered but a small inconvenience. "Lady Isabella, I do apologize."

"It was not your fault," she said, although her voice held a tremor. Whitmore slipped her back onto her feet, already missing the feel of her in his arms.

"Thank heaven," Lennox said, offering her his arm again. Whitmore wanted to strike him. Where the hell was the man going to take her? Walk her the rest of the way to Richmond? Even so, he forced himself to step aside and wait and see what his plan was.

Ravensmere was giving orders to the servants, directing repairs, his calm competence restoring order. The duchess moved back to her carriage, insisting to those who accompanied the party that Lady Isabella would be well.

Whitmore stood slightly apart, arms crossed, watching Isabella. She reassured the duchess, even laughed softly to dispel the worry in her sister's eyes, but he saw how her hands trembled when she thought no one was looking.

When the duke turned to him with a query about the horses, Whitmore answered absently. His focus never from her.

He didn't realize he'd spoken aloud until Ravensmere glanced sharply at him. "What was that?"

"I said," Whitmore replied, clearing his throat, "the road's uneven. Best not attempt to move the injured carriage until we've procured another wheel from town."

Ravensmere's brow furrowed, but before he could comment, Isabella swayed slightly. Whitmore took several quick steps and was beside her in an instant. "Easy," he said, gripping her elbows. "You've lost color."

"I'm fine," she whispered. "It was just—sudden, that is all."

"You're not fine." His tone came out sharper than intended, drawing attention from the others.

The duchess joined them. "Isabella?"

"She's well," Whitmore said quickly, lowering his voice. "Just shaken, but I believe she ought to return home."

He meant to step back then, but she wavered again, and instinct overruled propriety. He caught her fully, one arm around her waist steadying her. She gasped, her gloved hand clutching at his lapel.

Every eye was on them. He didn't care.

"Open the carriage door," he ordered a nearby footman. "The Ravensmere coach. Quickly, man."

The servant blinked at his tone but nodded. "Yes, yes, of course, my lord."

Hartley scooped Isabella up before she could protest, ignoring the startled murmurs that followed. She weighed nothing in his arms, her cheek brushing his shoulder as she whispered his name—soft, disbelieving.

"Put me down, Hartley," she murmured.

"Not a chance." His jaw was tight. "You're pale as death."

Her fingers curled weakly into his coat. "You'll start gossip."

"Let them talk," he said without hesitation. The words slipped out before he could recall them. He felt her breath hitch against his chest, and something in his heart twisted painfully.

When he reached the ducal coach, he set her gently on the ground, helping her climb in before following, crouching before her. The tiny cut on her temple had already dried, but he reached up again, brushing a loose curl from her face.

"Are you certain you're unharmed?"

She looked at him, her voice low. "You are making rather a scene."

"Good," he said. "Perhaps someone will finally believe I am capable of caring for more than myself."

Her lips parted slightly, but no sound came. The duchess's voice called from behind, brisk and readying the party to return to town, and the moment broke.

Whitmore left the vehicle and adjusted his coat. Ravensmere clapped him on the shoulder. "You've done us all a service, Whitmore. Thank you."

He nodded stiffly, turning away before anyone could read his face. His heart still pounded, his hands still tingled from the feel of her.

She was safe. That was all that mattered.

He told himself that as he mounted his horse, as the servants made ready to turn the party homeward. He told himself again when he saw her glance from the carriage window, meeting his eyes for the briefest instant before she looked away.

But even as he rode back to London, rain beginning to threaten once more, he knew the truth—he would never forget that moment. Not her blood on her temple. Not her name breaking from his throat before sense or propriety could stop him.

And certainly not the terrifying, unshakable knowledge he could have lost her, and it would have destroyed him.

CHAPTER TWENTY-ONE

Two days had passed since the accident on the way to Richmond, and though Isabella's bruises had faded, and her megrim had finally eased, her thoughts were far less settled.

She had spent the last forty-eight hours tucked away from the *ton*, refusing callers, sipping broth under Rosalind's watchful gaze, pretending that rest and quiet would calm her heart. It had not.

Every time she closed her eyes, she saw the carriage tilt, heard the crack of wood—and then, absurdly vivid, Whitmore's face as he tore open the door, his voice shouting her name as though she were the only soul alive worth saving.

He had looked terrified. Truly terrified and utterly charming all in one moment.

And then he had lifted her into his arms, heedless of who saw, as if he would fight the world rather than let her fall.

No, she had not forgotten. She doubted she ever could.

Now, as the Ravensmere carriage traveled toward the Theatre Royal, the city about them alive with light and carriages, she forced herself to look out at the crowded pavements instead of dwelling on the memory. Her sister sat opposite, speaking of the opera to come, while the duke read the bill of play by lamplight.

"It will be a fine evening," Rosalind said, adjusting her ear bobs. "Everyone of note shall be there, I hear."

"Everyone," Isabella murmured, wondering if that might include the man she had tried and failed to forget. She couldn't help but believe that now that he was imbedded in her skin, she'd never be rid of him.

But then, did she want to be? Increasingly she couldn't help but think she did not.

The carriage rolled to a stop before the theatre, the air hummed with expectation—the sharp scent of perfume and cigars floating in the breeze. Laughter echoed down the marble steps. Inside, candlelight shimmered on silk and muslin, illuminating both of London's echelons of society.

An usher guided them to the Ravensmere box, which afforded them a perfect view of the stage. Isabella stepped inside, smoothing her skirts, trying to appear composed. She was, after all, perfectly recovered. Entirely sensible. Utterly untroubled.

If only that were true...

She looked about the theater to the other boxes and the pit below. Lord Lennox was there, of course—polished, proper, and smiling up at her from his seat in the pit. He inclined his head with all the decorum of a gentleman. She returned the gesture, her pulse steady. Whatever she had thought of him before the accident, she saw now only predictability. A man who would never surprise her.

Never make her heart race or her body desire.

She sighed and continued to take in the theater. Several boxes beyond—and her breath caught.

Whitmore.

He sat alone in his family's box, his profile lit by the soft glow of a chandelier. His coat was perfectly cut, his cravat immaculate, but there was a weariness about his eyes that unsettled her. He wasn't watching the crowd or even the guests who clambered in to take their seats. No—he stared at the drawn velvet curtain on the stage as though lost in another world.

For a moment she drank in the sight of him like a woman desperate for water. She took in the slope of his shoulders, the stillness of him, and wondered what thoughts could darken a man who laughed at everything.

Then, as if her gaze had summoned him, he turned.

Their eyes met, held. The change in his face was instant and undeniable. The tension eased, the faint crease at his brow vanished, and a slow, unguarded smile spread over his lovely, wicked mouth.

Something fluttered deep in her stomach, and she knew to her very core everything had changed between them.

Rosalind, ever attuned to the goings on of her sisters cleared her throat. "You could go to him, if you wish," she murmured. "The marquess's box is close enough for me to chaperone from here, and we know him well. There would be no scandal in it."

Isabella hesitated. "Do you truly think so?"

"I think," her sister said, lips curving faintly, "that you want to."

Isabella looked again. He was still watching her, still looking at her hopefully as though he'd been holding his breath since Richmond and could finally exhale.

Perhaps she did want to.

She rose, smoothing her gown. "I shall only be a moment," she said, ignoring Rosalind's knowing look.

The duke barely noticed as she slipped from the box and descended the narrow corridor, the hum of conversation rising around her. Her heart beat far too quickly for such a simple errand. When she reached Whitmore's box, she paused at the curtained door just long enough to steady herself before stepping inside.

He stood at once, bowing deeply. "Lady Isabella."

"Lord Whitmore."

His eyes swept over her, lingering on her face. "You are well?"

"I am," she said. "Much better, thank you. The bruises are gone, and the only lasting mark is the worry I caused everyone."

"You frightened the life from me," he admitted quietly, and the raw honesty of it made her breath catch. "Forgive me. I meant—well, I am relieved to see you looking yourself again."

She smiled faintly, gloved fingers resting on the carved edge of a nearby chair. "You may keep the first version of your admission, my lord. I prefer truth to politeness."

His answering grin was brief but genuine. "Then I shall speak plainly. I've thought of little else but you since that day."

The words hung between them, dangerous and tender all at once. She wanted to tell him that she'd thought of nothing but him too, but instead, kept that admittance to herself.

He stepped closer, offering his hand. "Will you sit?"

She placed her hand in his. His fingers brushed the inside of her wrist as he helped her settle beside him, the touch sending an unexpected thrill through her.

"Your sister has forgiven me for the numerous missives I sent this week I hope?" he asked, attempting casualness, but she could see he was on edge. Wary and guarded on what he was saying and how he was acting around her.

Was she making him nervous? She hoped that was the case, for he certainly made her so. "I believe she has," Isabella said. "She mentioned you sent word several times, inquiring after my health."

He looked almost sheepish. "I did. Perhaps too many times."

"It was very kind." Her words were soft and hushed. "You were the only gentleman who did."

The murmur of conversation around them quietened as ushers entered the boxes to snuff out the sconces. One by one, the flames winked out until only the faint glow from the stage remained. Shadows cloaked the audience, the hush before the first note of music deepening the sense of intimacy.

Isabella became acutely aware of how close they sat. The rustle of his sleeve against her arm, the faint scent of sandalwood and something exclusively Hartley. Then, as the last lamp dimmed, his hand slid across her lap—seeking hers.

Her pulse leapt.

For a heartbeat she could not move, the dark concealing the tremor that ran through her. He didn't grip her tightly, only entwined their fingers and rested them on the seat between them, his thumb tracing a slow, comforting pattern along her glove.

She turned and met his gaze, the faint light from the stage catching his eyes.

"I have missed seeing you at events," he said quietly. "More than I can say."

Her throat tightened. This was not what she expected from Whitmore. He was a rake, a gentleman who loved nothing more than a lark, to tease and be teased. But this... This man wasn't anyone she recognized. He was earnest, looked at her with such longing that her body craved to drown in his green gaze. To listen to his sweet words and revel in them.

"We saw one another only two days ago." She tried to make light of his admission, but it did not change anything, and certainly seemed to have no bearing on him.

"And it has felt far longer than that," he murmured. "Too long. I've been worried, and I—" He stopped himself, exhaling. "I ache to be alone with you, Isabella. You have bedeviled me, and I cannot stop thinking of you."

The confession sent warmth flooding through

her. She had told herself his concern at Richmond was mere impulse, the gallantry of a man unaccustomed to seeing a woman hurt. But here, in the dark, she could hear the sincerity in his voice and while he may have rendered assistance to anyone, the fear she had read in his eyes two days before was wholly because he cared for her, and her alone.

"You should not say such things." She looked around, glad to see everyone was engrossed in the opera. "The Marquess of Whitmore does not declare such things. Certainly to a woman who is unmarried and of equal status."

His thumb stilled on her hand. "Perhaps it is time that I do?"

She smiled, though her heart pounded. This could not be real. He could not be declaring himself so freely. The orchestra struck its opening note, along with the soprano, a soft swell that rolled through the theater, but neither of them looked toward the stage.

"Are you saying that London's most scandalous rake has discovered what it is to...care?"

He tilted his head. "You think me incapable of such an emotion?"

"I think," she whispered, not wanting to hurt him, or make him believe she did not think he could come to love. But to be vulnerable with him was not an easy step to take. "You are trying."

He gave a quiet laugh, but it sounded pained. He turned toward her, his hold increasing on her hand. "You know what I was before," he said. "You've heard the stories. Half of them are true."

"Half." *More like all.*

"I cannot imagine any more trysts unless they all involve one particular lady whom I call Bells."

Her pulse fluttered and she swallowed. "Hartley." They were so close, leaning toward each other as if they could not bear to be apart. Her gaze dipped to his lips. She wanted his mouth on her. She wanted him to touch her, to make her sing with as much passion as the woman on stage.

The opera continued—voices soaring, music spilling from the stage in waves of sound—but it seemed far away, a dream beyond the little box they shared. Every note was a pulse that matched the rhythm of her heart.

She tried to focus on the performance, on anything, but realization struck her with such force that it left her senseless.

She was falling in love with him. No sooner did she have the thought did she dismiss it. No, she wasn't falling whatsoever. She'd already fallen and landed with a thump at this man's feet.

His breath brushed her ear. "You should leave before I steal you away and we become the talk of the *ton*," he whispered. "I'd like nothing more than to be alone with you and out of sight from this society."

"And what would you do if we were to steal away?" She bit her bottom lip, watching the array of emotions flutter over his handsome face. The determination, the desire, the heat that settled on his handsome features left her adjusting her seat. She ached, wanted him so much she could feel the telltale dampness between her legs.

"It would mean my reputation would be in tatters and we'd be married within three days."

"It would," he said, his voice a deep purr.

The curtain to the box opened and a slither of light illuminated them. "Dearest, we thought we might join you instead of sitting separately."

Isabella and Hartley both moved to gain space between them. Her sister and brother-in-law settled behind them, a presence that told her that perhaps their intimate discussion had caused whispers she'd not been aware of. It was just like Rosalind to come and ensure her reputation wasn't ruined.

What would the duchess say if she knew only a moment before Isabella was contemplating stealing away with Whitmore? To be alone with him like they both wished.

The music swelled. She could feel the heat of him beside her, the slow rise and fall of his breath. Her mind whispered warnings—what society would say if she continued to act without thought, what her sister would think should she be careless—but her body betrayed her with its every tremor.

She closed her eyes, her hands tightening in her lap, and she knew in that moment that she could not give a tinkers damn what anyone thought.

Right now, she merely wished to live.

CHAPTER
TWENTY-TWO

The theater had emptied hours ago, and the echoes of song and applause still lingered in Whitmore's mind. At intermission, he had covertly slipped a small, folded note into Isabella's gloved hand. He'd told her not to read it until she was home safe in her room—and to burn it straight after.

He was playing a dangerous game, one that had no clear ending. Yet he knew one thing with absolute certainty—he had to see her again, alone.

He needed to kiss her, even if that was all she would ever allow him.

The night was cold, the air thick with fog as he waited across Grosvenor Square. His coach stood beneath the shadow of a towering elm, the horses restless and snorting in the silence. The hour had long passed two. The city slept, yet the pulse in his chest refused to quiet.

He kept his gaze fixed on the small side gate of the ducal townhouse. Any moment now—

And then, as though the darkness itself had conjured her, she appeared.

Isabella slipped from the shadows, her dark cloak drawn tight, her hood low. The faint lamplight brushed her cheek, revealing the delicate hue of her skin, the nervous glance she cast about before hurrying forward. His driver saw her and instantly moved the carriage closer.

Within seconds of her stepping free of the garden gate, Whitmore had opened the door. She slipped inside, a whisper of silk and rose filling the air between them. The coachman clucked softly to the horses, and they rolled away, leaving only the sound of wheels on damp cobblestone behind.

No words passed between them. There was no need.

Whitmore reached for her the moment she entered. Their mouths met, urgent and claiming, and every shred of restraint he had fought to keep disintegrated.

Her lips parted, a soft needy sound escaping her, and he deepened the kiss, his hand sliding into her hair, tilting her face to his. Her scent enveloped him, and it was all he could do not to lose himself completely.

The kiss grew fierce, the kind that left little thought behind. She pressed closer, her body fitting perfectly against his. The heat of her chest burned through the thin barrier of his coat. He had kissed women before—dozens, perhaps more—but none had ever made him feel as though his heart had been stolen from his chest.

The world outside ceased to exist. There was only her mouth, her breath, her trembling hands clutching at him as if she too were caught in the storm of it.

She was magic in his arms. He was undone.

Desire clawed through him, sharp and wild, demanding he take what she offered. Yet even as she arched closer, he fought for control, fought not to shatter what remained of his reason. He was hard, aching, consumed.

He had never wanted like this.

He had never wanted *her* like this—because to want her was to risk everything. Her lips moved against his throat, her fingers slipping down the front of his waistcoat, skimming the fabric of his breeches. His heart stopped, his breath caught.

"Isabella..." he rasped, half warning, half plea.

But she silenced him with another kiss, soft and devastating.

The question hovered on his tongue, the one that would change everything between them if he dared speak it aloud. It lived there, alongside the truth he could no longer deny. He loved her, wanted to marry her.

To say such a thing aloud would undo him entirely. It would make him hers, body and soul, and he feared that once she saw him clearly—past the witticisms, the sullied reputation, the careless rake she believed him to be—she would recoil.

He had made a personality of laughter, of living as if nothing touched him, but she affected him. God help him, she reached the parts of him that had never seen the light.

Isabella's low groan pulled him from his thoughts. She kissed him again, hungrier now, her hands exploring as though she sought to commit every inch of him to memory. He groaned too, matching her pace, his body straining to keep from taking her here and now.

Control slipped, fragile and fleeting.

Her hand pressed against him through the fall of his breeches, and he froze, the pleasure and torment of it flooding through him. His body burned, his mind reeled.

"Isabella," he said again, his voice a hoarse whisper. "You must stop."

"I do not wish to stop," she whispered back, her breath hot against his ear.

He shut his eyes, his head falling forward until his forehead met hers. "You have no idea what you're doing to me."

She smiled, and it was his undoing. "I want you, Hartley."

The words shattered him.

A stronger man would have denied her. But Whitmore had never claimed to be strong. He had spent years giving in to his every vice, and now, faced with the only woman who had ever made him question himself, he found he had no strength left to resist.

He caught her face in his hands, kissing her again—deep, desperate, reverent. He wanted to brand her, to make her remember this moment as fiercely as he would. With a growl of surrender, he lifted her onto his lap, the motion drawing a gasp from her throat.

Her cloak slipped, revealing pale skin, the faintest glimpse of the curve where her dress had loosened. His mouth followed instinct before reason intervened, tracing the line of her neck, the fluttering pulse beneath her jaw.

She trembled, her hands finding his shoulders, pulling him close. The carriage rocked gently, the sound of rain beginning to patter against the roof, drumming in rhythm with the frantic beat of his heart. The city outside might as well have ceased to exist.

He could have her now. One tug at her bodice, lifting of her silken skirts, one whispered word, and she would be his. But the thought struck him cold—because he didn't want her like that. Not here, not like this.

He wanted all of her.

He wanted her laughter in the morning, her scent on his pillows, her name tied to his forever. God help him. He wanted her as his wife.

He stilled, his breath ragged, and buried his face against her throat. She sighed, her fingers threading into his hair. "Hartley," she murmured, her voice soft, full of trust.

That broke him completely. He lifted his head, eyes meeting hers in the dim light. "You have no idea what you ask of me."

"I ask for nothing," she said. "I only want you."

He kissed her again because words were useless now. The taste of her was salt and sweetness, fire and ruin. Every touch carried both promise and warning. His hands trembled as they skimmed the silk of her gown, feeling the rapid rise and fall of her chest. He forced himself to stop before he crossed the point of no return.

"I cannot," he whispered against her lips.

She blinked, her eyes wide. "Cannot?"

"Not like this," he said softly. "You deserve better than a scoundrel in a carriage at dawn."

She studied him, her chest rising with each unsteady breath. "This does not feel so sullied as those words."

He gave a low, rough laugh. "It feels like madness."

The carriage slowed, the rhythmic clatter of hooves easing to a halt. Whitmore glanced out the window and realized, with a twist of fate, that they were near his townhouse. He reached for her hand and pressed a lingering kiss to her knuckles. "Come inside with me, Bells. Before I change my mind."

She hesitated only a moment before leaning forward, brushing a feather-light kiss against his mouth. "I would like that very much."

So would he.

Within minutes of her agreement, they slipped inside his house, the hush of sleeping servants wrapping around them like a secret. No one stirred. His staff was long to bed—a longstanding order, since he was rarely home before dawn.

He didn't bother with the rear entrance but drew her through the front and up the grand staircase, their fingers twined, the urgency between them building with every step. The air was thick with want, the faint scent of rain and candle wax mingling as they moved.

They barely reached his suite before he closed the door and pulled her into his arms. His mouth found hers, deep and claiming, and she melted against him. Here—in his home, in his arms—everything he'd tried to resist came undone.

She denied him nothing, her touch as eager as his. Their clothing soon littered the floor—stockings, gloves, gowns, and coats forming a careless trail to the bed. The firelight painted their skin gold, shadows dancing across the walls like silent witnesses.

Hartley came over her, his body hard and eager. He lifted her leg to hook over his hip before lowering himself, pausing to take in the sight of her. Hair unpinned, eyes heavy with desire—she was an undeniable temptress.

He reached between them, brushed his hand over her soft curls and down to her slick heat. She trembled beneath him, arching into his touch, her breath catching.

"You're so beautiful," he murmured.

Her fingers curled in his hair, tugging him down for a kiss. He went willingly, aligning their bodies, his control slipping as she opened to him like a flower in bloom. She did not flinch or turn away, understood what they were doing, what it meant—and in that moment, so did he.

She was his. He was hers. And the world beyond this room ceased to exist.

He pressed into her, and she met him with a gasp, clutching at his shoulders. "I want you so much, Hartley."

Her plea broke him. He thrust into her, taking her innocence—and something far more precious—with that single, irrevocable move. She wrapped her legs around him, kissed him with fierce abandon, and he thought he might lose himself entirely.

Every breath was a struggle for control. Every movement a prayer that she found pleasure in his touch. She stirred beneath him with instinctive grace, her body rising to meet his, soft sighs escaping with each roll of her hips.

It was too much—too perfect.

"Yes, Hartley," she whispered, her voice a trembling appeal.

Her body tightened around him, and he felt her release crest and break. Her soft cry tore through the quiet room, dragging him down with her. "Oh yes, Bells."

They came together, clinging, shaking, their bodies shuddering with shared ecstasy. When the tremors eased, he kissed her again, a tender press of lips that spoke of everything he dared not say aloud.

He drew her close, her body warm and pliant in his arms. She tucked herself against his side, her breathing slowing until the rhythm matched his own.

"That was sensational," she whispered, glancing up at him.

His heart gave a foolish tumble. To have her here, in his bed, felt like the only right thing in the world. Tomorrow, he would take her home to Ravensmere and ask for her hand. After the banns were called, Lady Isabella would be his—his wife, his everything.

"I aim to please my lady—always."

She laughed softly and pressed a kiss to his chest, sending a rush of warmth through him. "I do not think I shall ever be able to walk again. My legs feel like jelly."

"I'm glad to hear it. Now you cannot run away." He reached down and tickled her until she squealed, then pulled her close again, his grin fading as her hand rose to cradle his jaw.

"I do not ever wish for the night to end," she whispered.

He kissed the crown of her head, his voice low and certain. "Nor I."

Tomorrow, he would speak to Ravensmere. Tomorrow, everything would change. Tonight, though, she was in his arms—and for the first time in his life, Hartley thought that forever might not be long enough.

CHAPTER TWENTY-THREE

Isabella was able to sneak home without being caught in the early hours of the morning. Although she heard an under maid in the ducal library setting the fires, she managed to slip upstairs undetected and jump into bed.

She gained an hour or two of sleep before her lady's maid arrived with the usual hot chocolate and hot water. As she dressed and prepared for the day, memories of the night before swirled in her mind, a mix of disbelief and longing.

After what had happened with Hartley, how might her life change?

Would he attend the Oliver ball this evening? Would there be an opportunity for them to sneak away and be alone?

She longed to see him already, though only a few hours had passed.

Collecting her gloves and bonnet, in the mood for a walk, she exited her room—only to skid to a halt at the top of the stairs when raised voices met her ears.

She froze, listening for several heartbeats,

trying to make sense of the commotion. Then recognition struck. Was that Hartley and Ravensmere shouting at each other? The sound of a fist slamming against wood echoed up the stairwell and startled her.

She looked along the corridor to where one of the maids had stopped dusting a sideboard, wide-eyed. Isabella gathered her skirts and hurried downstairs, her heart thudding with every step.

What was Hartley doing here? Why were they arguing?

She paused midstep. Could he be here to ask for her hand? They had not spoken of marriage, but he was a gentleman. Perhaps he thought it right to come this morning, to make a formal request after what had occurred between them.

Would she marry him merely because she had been in his bed?

Her hand flew to her stomach, a wave of cold fear rippling through her. The possibility that she might be carrying his child—though not a thought that had entered her mind the night before—was an outcome that could ruin her and her family.

She swallowed the bile rising in her throat. Of course, she would marry him if that were the case, even if it were not a love match. But for her, at least, it was absolutely that emotion.

She loved him.

Could not have given herself to a man she did not adore, and she adored Hartley. As much as he had infuriated her at the start of the Season, pressed her buttons in all the wrong way, aggravated and annoyed her, now the thought of being without him felt unbearable.

Her sister's voice carried into the hall, confirming there were three in the library. Without knocking, Isabella pushed open the door. The duke and duchess stood behind the desk, Whitmore before it. All three were red-faced, the air thick with tension.

"What is the meaning of this?" she demanded, closing the door firmly behind her. "The entire house can hear you shouting. What is going on?"

Hartley's eyes met hers. His expression softened, but he was clearly in high color, and it was obvious he and Ravensmere had been quarreling.

"Isabella, darling," Rosalind said, coming around the desk to take her hand. "London is rife this morning with talk."

Isabella didn't dare speak. Had someone seen her steal into the marquess's carriage last night? Was she the latest on-dit? Had she ruined herself—and by extension, her family?

Her knees felt weak, and she sank into a nearby chair.

Still, she could not bring herself to ask.

Whitmore remained silent, glaring at the duke, who glowered right back.

"Isabella," Rosalind began, visibly shaken. "News has spread that the Duke of Rolle's betrothal to Miss Wilson is no more. She has called it off and created quite the scandal. Both families are in disarray trying to repair their reputations. But it is the reason for the broken engagement that has the *ton's* tongues wagging."

Isabella nodded slowly, still not understanding how that could have led to this morning's quarrel. "I am very sorry for His Grace and Miss Wilson, but what has that to do with us? Why is everyone so out of sorts here?"

Rosalind returned to her husband's side and exchanged a grim look with him before continuing. "It is said that Miss Wilson attended supper with the duke at a ball last evening. He was in his cups—quite foxed, from all accounts—and very loose with his tongue. He let it slip, in conversation with Miss Wilson and several of their friends, that he and the Marquess of Whitmore had entered into a bet at the beginning of the Season, at the Kenworthy Ball to be exact. A thousand-pound wager."

Her sister hesitated, then forced more words out. "A stake to see which of them could gain favor with you, Isabella. Or rather, which of them could steal your first kiss."

Isabella gasped and the room spun. Her pulse roared in her ears and she was certain she hadn't heard right.

No. Whitmore would not be so cruel...

Rosalind's voice wavered. "The duke went on to boast that Whitmore had won the bet—and he was put out that he owed a thousand pounds for never having the pleasure."

The pleasure.

Her pleasure.

The words tore through her like a knife.

Had the whole of London been laughing behind her back? Had Whitmore thought her a lark, so desperate that she would succumb to his false charms? Heat rushed to her cheeks, knowing that was exactly what had occurred. She had fallen for his pretty words, and wicked mouth.

Fool.

"Miss Wilson left the supper room at once, quite distressed from all accounts," Rosalind explained. "Her father sent word that the engagement was off. Stated that the duke's cruel words toward you, dearest had shamed not only his betrothed but every young lady in society." She paused. "They have since fled back to Bath, while the duke himself has retreated to Wesley Hall, where he will no doubt lick his wounds."

Isabella turned to Whitmore.

He looked at her, shame etched into every line of his handsome, brutal face. "It was all a lie?" she asked quietly, though her voice trembled. "Everything you said—everything you made me believe—was a falsehood?"

"Isabella, no," he said, reaching for her. She flinched, and he stopped his attempt to touch her. "Yes, there was a bet," he admitted, his voice thick with regret. "But it was not long before I realized I teased and tempted you of my own free will. What I began to feel for you was not because I wanted to win a thousand pounds, in fact I instructed the duke that I would not accept the funds. I swear to you, Isabella. It wasn't long before the idea of the duke or anyone anywhere near you made me crazed. No bet could make me care for you, only you were capable of that, and you won me. I love you, so very much."

She stared at him, the ringing in her ears deafening. If she stood, she was certain she would faint. "How many people knew of this stake between you and the duke?" she whispered. "How many laughed at me while you both courted me? And here I was thinking that for once, my Season might finally be a success, and all the while, I was a joke."

She covered her mouth with her hand, bile rising in her throat. "And now everyone knows it. All our friends and family, everyone. My reputation is ruined." Her voice cracked at the words and she gasped, unable to hold the realization at bay.

Rosalind reached for her, but Isabella shook her head. "I am ruined," she said hoarsely. "I will never marry now."

"My dearest, please do not cry," Rosalind murmured, casting Whitmore a furious look.

Ravensmere's face hardened to stone. "You will marry her, Whitmore," her brother-in-law's voice was like ice.

Isabella flinched. "I will not marry him. I'd rather be ruined than marry him."

"There is no choice," Rosalind said gently. "You must marry him, darling. We must salvage what we can of your reputation. Everyone knows Whitmore has kissed you—you know how such things are viewed."

Isabella's jaw clenched. She would not confess that she had done far worse than kiss his lordship. She had given him her body, her heart, her trust—believing he loved her.

She turned to him, her voice shaking. "How dare you."

"Isabella," he said, anguish in his eyes. "I came here this morning to ask for your hand *before* any of this became known. That should tell you the wager had nothing to do with my proposal. I love you. I want you to be the next Marchioness of Whitmore. Please, let me explain."

She shook her head, tears blurring her vision. "I do not want to hear any of your excuses." She blinked rapidly, but the tears slipped free, heavy and hot against her cheeks. She swiped them away angrily, though more followed.

Rosalind's eyes shone with pity. "You must marry Whitmore, darling. And let us hope that, in time, he will do everything in his power to make amends for this cruelty."

Whitmore faced the duke and duchess. "Your Graces, I never meant to hurt Lady Isabella. No matter what has been said today, I came here to ask for her hand, as you well know, *before* any of this was made aware to me. I love Isabella, and I will spend my life trying to make her happy."

"I do not want you to make me happy," Isabella snapped. "And while I may be forced to marry you, you will be fortunate if I can look upon you again without loathing."

"Bells, please—"

"I have heard enough." She stood, her voice devoid of warmth. "I am going to my room. Do not call on me again until the day of our marriage. I will not see you before then."

She left, her skirts whispering across the floor, leaving her sister and brother-in-law to finalize whatever arrangements were to be made with Whitmore's family.

She wanted no part of it.

No part of him.

And none of the man who had stolen her heart—and shattered it in one cruel wager.

CHAPTER

TWENTY-FOUR

Hartley stood in the middle of his study, the morning light striking the decanter on his desk. His coat was unbuttoned, his cravat askew, and his hair a disheveled mess from running his fingers through it for the better part of an hour.

He had tried to drink, but the liquor turned to ash on his tongue. He had tried to pace, but his legs felt heavy, his chest tight.

Isabella's eyes haunted him—wide and full of betrayal.

He pressed a hand to his forehead. "God, what have I done?"

He had gone to the Ravensmere House that morning with the best of intentions. He would speak to the duke, ask for Isabella's hand, and set things right. He had rehearsed the words, imagined her shy smile, the warmth in her gaze when he offered for her. Asked her to love him as much as he loved her.

Then everything had gone to hell.

The duke's fury, Rosalind's cold disapproval,

Isabella's tears—it was a nightmare he could not wake from.

He moved to the window, looking out onto Berkely Square. The world outside went on as usual. Carriages rolled past, gentlemen tipped their hats, ladies took the air. No one knew that his life had just come undone.

And worse—he had undone hers as well.

He closed his eyes and saw her again as she had been the morning before. Her hair loose around her shoulders, her lips parted beneath his. She had given him everything, and he had ruined her in return.

A wager.

A foolish, hurtful wager made in haste, meant to irritate his nemesis. Never once had he believed it would lead to the overwhelming affection he had for Isabella. The one woman who refused to be swayed by his charms and yet had won his heart with her wit and sweetness. He was privileged to have won her affection and trust in return, and yet he'd thrown everything she held dear back in her face like it did not matter. Or at least that was what she would now believe.

The image of her hearing the truth—of her face crumpling in disbelief—would haunt him until the day he died.

He sank into his chair, resting his head in his hands.

"She will never forgive me."

There was a knock at the door, and his butler entered quietly. "My lord, are you unwell?"

"No, only a fool."

The man hesitated, unsure if he should remain in his presence. "Shall I bring coffee?"

Hartley shook his head. A flintlock might serve him better... Hartley shook his head and leaned back in his chair and closed his eyes, knowing that such dark thoughts were not welcome or helpful. He groaned, dragging both hands down his face. He had always fancied himself a man who could charm his way out of trouble. But this—this went beyond either.

He had destroyed the one person who had seen good in him.

His gaze fell to the desk where a small box lay—the ring he had chosen for her, a delicate gold band set with a emerald the same color as her eyes. He picked it up, turning it in his fingers.

He had planned to give it to her yesterday, to ask her to be his wife, not out of duty or scandal, but because he wanted to wake every day for the rest of his life and see her face.

Now that dream seemed laughable. Unattainable. She would never forgive him.

"She will marry me because she must," he whispered. "And she will hate me every day for it."

He rose, pacing to the hearth. The fire had long gone cold, the ash gray and lifeless. It mirrored how he felt—spent, hollow, and beyond repair. He thought of leaving London, of disappearing to his estate in Kent until the wedding. But he could not. To vanish now would brand Isabella forever, and he needed this time to make amends. To try to salvage something of what they had started.

He would face the shame, the gossip, the pity. He would do it for her.

Because he loved her.

God help him, he loved her.

The admission struck him hard, leaving him breathless. He sank into the chair once more, the ring clenched in his fist. He did not deserve her forgiveness, but he would earn it all the same. He would marry her. Protect her. Make her smile again —one day.

And if she never loved him in return, that would be his penance. Hartley lifted his gaze toward the window, where the faintest glimmer of sunlight pierced the gray clouds.

"Tomorrow," he murmured. "Tomorrow I will make it right."

He had broken the only woman he had ever loved. Now he would spend the rest of his life trying to piece her back together.

CHAPTER TWENTY-FIVE

Isabella shut the door to her chamber and leaned against it, her pulse pounding so violently she feared her heart might burst. The echo of their voices still haunted the hall below—her sister's pitying tone, Ravensmere's fury, Hartley's desperate insistence that he loved her. The words replayed again and again, as sharp as the morning light bleeding through the curtains.

Her love had been a wager.

Her heart, a game.

She pressed a trembling hand to her chest, feeling the ache settle deep into her ribs. "How could you," she whispered to the empty room.

Her maid, hearing her enter, had started forward to offer assistance, but one look at Isabella's pale face and red-rimmed eyes sent the girl scurrying out again. Good. She wanted no witness to this humiliation.

Crossing to the bed, Isabella sank onto the edge, her knees weak. She stared at her reflection in the mirror—her hair tumbling down in soft curls, her eyes rimmed with tears—and barely recognized the woman staring back.

A woman who had given everything to a man she believed loved her. A man who had laughed behind her back. What a fool she had been.

She wiped her face, but fresh tears slipped down her cheeks. Her gown felt suffocating, the stays too tight, the air too thick. She took a deep breath, trying to calm her nerves, but she knew nothing could calm her right now. Nothing could make what had happened right.

The house stirred below. Somewhere in the distance, Rosalind was giving orders, her calm voice covering what must have been chaos in the household. Word would spread fast—by afternoon, every drawing room in London would be abuzz with her name. Lady Isabella Ravensmere, the girl who lost her virtue to a wager, or near enough. A kiss was seen as just as scandalous as giving herself to a man without the security of marriage. The thought that she'd done that also made her skin crawl and she couldn't believe she'd been so foolish.

She closed her eyes.

Hartley's touch burned on her skin. His voice, the way he had whispered her name as if it meant something sacred, still echoed in her ear. And to think she had woken this morning wondering if he would call, if he would ask for her hand as a man in love, not one cornered by scandal.

And now she must marry him or be ruined, the thought as bitter as salt on her tongue. How could she be so foolish as to believe him his words. Her heart squeezed painfully.

Would she ever look at him again and not see

the deception? Exhaustion consumed her, but not wanting to give in to despair, she pushed away from the bed, pacing to the window. The sky outside was pale and washed, as though even the morning had no color left to offer her.

Below, the duke's carriage rolled from the mews. Had Hartley also left? Was he already home, trying to come up with another farce of a lie that would win her heart. Win her trust again.

She scoffed at the thought. Nothing would ever repair the damage that he had done. A knock came at her door, before Rosalind's soft voice followed. "Isabella, may I come in?"

Isabella's throat closed, but she managed a quiet, "Yes."

Her sister entered, closing the door behind her. She crossed the room and stood with her beside the window. "You know we are only thinking of your future, darling. We must protect your name."

"I know." Isabella's voice broke on the words. "But I cannot marry a man who made me the subject of a bet. It would be bad enough should I only have found out about it, but our friends, soon our family will hear of it. The shame that he married me because Ravensmere found out about our kiss is too humiliating for words. Everyone will know he does not love me, no one will ever believe otherwise."

Rosalind took her in her arms and held her close. "He came to ask for your hand before the news broke. I saw it in his face the sincerity and care he has for you. No matter how angry I am at him, I do truly think he meant to make you his wife."

Isabella shook her head, tears gathering anew. "He meant to save himself. He always has. I thought him changed—that he'd left behind the rakish fool everyone has witnessed for years, but he hasn't. He's just cleverer at hiding it."

Rosalind squeezed her tighter before pulling back. "You must decide what you want from this. If you cannot forgive him now, you will have to learn to live beside him in civility. That is what society requires, even if it is not what I wish for you."

Isabella managed a small, hollow laugh. "Civility. I wonder if I have any of that left."

Rosalind reached out and smoothed Isabella's hair from her face. "Rest today, think things through and plan. You will need your strength in the coming weeks."

When her sister left, Isabella curled onto the bed, drawing the covers over herself. Sleep eluded her, but she closed her eyes anyway, as if shutting out the daylight could banish the truth that her future was no longer her own.

CHAPTER TWENTY-SIX

Isabella managed to evade Whitmore for three weeks. Each Sunday came and went, ticking down her time, as the banns were called, and the day drew nearer when she would become the Marchioness of Whitmore.

Her stomach had not stopped churning at the thought of having to move into his home, to live under the same roof as the man who had broken her heart. Even the mere mention of his name made her pulse skip, not from affection, but from the bitter taste of betrayal that clung to her tongue.

How was she to look at him after what he had done?

When she had first thought him sincere—believing his attentions meant friendship and, later, something deeper—he had already been deceiving her. What kind of man tricked a woman into feeling something he himself never intended to offer?

Whitmore was no friend of hers.

He had made her look a fool before society, and she could not forgive him for it.

Over the past three weeks, she had re-entered

society with her head held high, the Duke and Duchess of Ravensmere at her side offering strength and protection. Few dared speak ill in front of her, not with her brother-in-law's stern gaze cutting through a room, but Isabella saw the laughter in people's eyes. The flutter of ladies' fans, which whispers hid behind, the subtle tilt of a gentleman's head as he murmured to his companion—she knew they spoke of her. Pity and near ruin clung to her like a faint, unwanted perfume.

They speculated about what kind of future she could possibly have with one of London's most notorious rakes—a man forced to marry because of his own folly. It was what everyone said, including herself.

His affections had been untrue. It had all been a lie. But at least he had his thousand pounds...

The thought made her fists curl in her lap, and she very nearly struck the velvet seat of the carriage as it rattled along the cobblestones toward their night's entertainment. The rhythmic jostle of the wheels and the faint scent of the horses outside only fueled her agitation.

Tonight would be the first time she would see Whitmore since that disastrous morning in Ravensmere's study. There would be no escaping him in such company. How was she to stand beside him before the *ton*, pretend that nothing had happened, that she was content?

She was not.

Isabella stared out the carriage window, the city flickering past in lantern-lit blurs. Thankfully, Rosalind and the duke did not attempt conversation. They had learned these past weeks that her temper and sorrow were best left alone unless she engaged with them first. Isabella had grown curt in her replies, short-tempered, not from malice but from disappointment in herself—for falling for a man she should never have trusted.

Damn him.

The carriage rolled to a stop before the grand London home, its façade blazing with light. A footman stepped forward, opening the door and setting down the steps.

"Ready, my dear?" Rosalind asked softly.

"As I shall ever be," Isabella murmured, gathering her skirts.

Inside, the air was warm and scented with beeswax. Thankfully, society did not hush at their arrival as it had at previous events. Instead the orchestra played on, couples glided across the floor, and laughter carried on under the golden glow of chandeliers.

They walked along the edge of the ballroom until Rosalind stopped near Lady Whiteley, one of her friends. Isabella stood at their side, smiling politely though her mind was elsewhere.

The hairs at the back of her neck prickled, the air shifting as if the very room acknowledged his presence. She knew who it was before she even turned to look. Her breath caught.

Whitmore.

He moved through the crowd with unhurried grace, every step measured. Guests parted for him without hesitation, as though some unspoken command was uttered from his lips, and they obeyed. The candlelight burnished his dark hair, caught the cut of his jaw, and she despised how her heart stilled at the sight of the handsome cur.

She wanted to strike him. She wanted to rip that beautiful mask from his face, to make him hurt as she was. But she could not. Instead, she had to smile, to pretend happiness where there was none.

"Your Graces," Whitmore said with an elegant bow before turning to her. He took her gloved hand and brushed his lips across her knuckles. She ignored the jump in her pulse, the warmth that rushed through her despite herself. Her heart refused to accept the cruelty he was capable of.

"Bells," he murmured, stepping close enough that she caught the faint scent of his cologne. He pressed a kiss to her cheek for a moment, she almost forgot her character. Her body swayed toward him before her mind caught up and screamed *no*.

His hand tightened slightly on hers, keeping her in place. "We need to talk," he whispered. "It has been too long, Isabella."

She stepped back, freeing her hand from his grasp. She could not let him touch her. Her body might betray her, but her mind would not. "There is nothing left to say," she said, smiling brightly as a passing couple drifted near. "We are betrothed, married in a week. Tonight we must pretend that all is well."

She lifted her chin, smiling up at him, though her gaze was ice. The flicker of pain that crossed his eyes pleased her more than it should.

"Isabella," he said softly, "it may have started as a wager, but please know that it soon altered for me. I did not care if I won or lost. All I cared about was you. I would not have persisted after that first kiss had I not wanted more. Had I not thought that for the first time in my life, I had met someone I was falling in love with."

She forced a smile, though his words struck deep. "*Loved*, my lord? Are we at past tense already?" Her voice trembled despite her best effort to sound composed. "I will do my duty and marry you to save my reputation and yours. But I do not think we can return to what I once believed we had."

"We can," he said quickly. The plea in his voice twisted something inside her. She wanted to shut her heart against him, to lock him out completely. Why was it so hard?

"Isabella." He took her arm and led her a few steps away, toward the shadow of a column, affording them a sliver of privacy. "I was in Ravensmere's office that morning to ask for your hand. It was only after I had asked permission that the duke informed me of what was afoot about town. If my feelings for you were insincere, would I have gone to him? I wanted to marry you before any of this became public. I love you. I love you so much. Please—"

She swallowed the lump in her throat. She had replayed that morning countless times, imagining how it might have gone differently. His arrival at her home *did* play in his favor, but she could not shake the thought that it was merely duty that drove him—because they had shared a bed.

Even now, the memory of his touch made her skin warm, and her stomach tighten in shame and longing alike. "Your request for my hand," she said quietly, "may have been due to the...necessity of the situation, not because of love. You needed to offer for the woman whose virtue you compromised."

"I did not offer because you gave yourself to me," he said fiercely. "I want you as my wife, in every sense. I want you in my bed, in my life, at my side. Please, Isabella."

She could not bear another word. "If you'll excuse me," she whispered, her throat tight. "I must get away from you."

She turned, moving swiftly toward the doors, her pulse hammering. The ballroom's heat pressed in, the music suddenly too loud, the laughter too sharp against her ears. Her vision swam.

"Isabella, wait," he called after her.

She ignored him, her skirts brushing against her ankles as she quickened her pace. Guests turned to look as she passed, murmuring, whispering behind gloved hands. By the time she reached the front hall, her lungs burned. A footman sprang forward to open the door, the night air outside cool and damp, a welcome reprieve.

"Have the Ravensmere carriage brought round," she said breathlessly.

Whitmore caught up to her as the vehicle rolled forward, the lamps glinting against the polished black panels.

"I cannot let you go like this," he said, his tone rough, desperation bleeding through his carefully schooled mask.

"You already have," she said, stepping inside before he could offer a hand.

He followed, closing the door behind them. The latch clicked, sealing them in the dim, private space. "Get out." She pointed to the door, but he did not move.

Instead, the carriage jolted forward. Soon the steady rhythm of hooves struck against the cobblestones. They sat in silence, the space between them thick with all that had been said—and all that hadn't.

Isabella stared out the small window, refusing to meet his gaze. Her reflection trembled in the glass, her eyes glistening. The faint warmth of his nearness reached her still, stirring feelings she despised herself for having.

Whitmore's hand flexed on his knee, as though he longed to reach for her. But he did not.

Probably wise. For right at this moment, she wasn't sure she wouldn't hurt him if he did. Her body thrummed with anger and confusion, her palms pressed tightly together in her lap to stop them from trembling.

"I beg you, Bells, forgive me," he said, voice low and ragged. "I know it may seem as though what I agreed to with Rolle is unforgivable—a trust broken that cannot be repaired—but I promise you, I have never felt anything like what I feel for you with anyone. You haunt my every thought. For you, and you alone, I plan and hope. I think of a future for us together, traveling, living at our estates, having children, a life that I've never allowed myself to believe I could have."

She watched him, startled by how raw and unguarded he sounded. She hadn't thought him capable of such honesty. There was a rough edge to his tone that caught somewhere deep in her chest, an ache she didn't want to feel.

He slipped from the seat opposite her and knelt before her, clasping her legs in a pleading way that made her breath catch. They hadn't been this close in weeks. His warmth reached through the fabric of her skirts, unsettling her. His scent—sandalwood, and the faintest trace of brandy—filled the air and brought a rush of memories she wished she could forget.

It was dangerous, having him this near. Too testing to her resolve, too tempting to the parts of her heart she was trying to harden.

"I've always hidden behind a mask of mischief," he said, his voice steadier now but still quiet. "It's probably why Rolle requested the wager from me and no one else. He knew I wouldn't deny it, especially when it involved you. Perhaps he picked up on my interest in you, even then. Whether you'll admit it or not, there's always been a trigger between us. When I had the excuse to try to make you kiss me, I couldn't let it go. I wanted to kiss you, Isabella. I wanted you to be mine. I hated the duke attempting the same and was more than pleased when his attentions moved to Miss Wilson, for it left me free to court you—to make you love me as much as I fell in love with you."

She tried to ignore his pretty, practiced words, but they slipped past her defenses anyway. Each word settled like a small, treacherous ember in her chest, glowing faintly against the cold weight of her anger.

He leaned closer, his eyes searching hers. The movement was so small, so tender, that she didn't realize how little space was left between them until she could feel his breath on her lips.

"Please, Bells," he whispered. "Please forgive me. I cannot live without you."

Her breath hitched. The sincerity in his gaze twisted something inside her, and for one awful moment, she almost believed him.

But then she remembered.

"You cannot say such things to me and expect that I'll forget the wager," she said, her voice shaking despite her best efforts to keep it calm. "You made a fool of me before all of London, Hartley. You broke my trust. That cannot simply be undone by words whispered in a shadowed carriage."

"I know," he said softly, his gaze never leaving her. "But I would give anything to make it right. You are the only person who has ever seen the man I could be, not the scoundrel the world believes me to be."

She wanted to look away, to stop seeing the pain etched on his handsome face. Her throat tightened, and she pressed her lips together, forcing her composure.

"Your remorse changes nothing," she said quietly. "You lied. You betrayed me. And though you may think yourself in love, you are not. Your disappointment will pass, just as mine will and we shall make the best of this farce of a marriage to come."

He exhaled harshly, still on his knees before her. His head bowed, and she could see the tremor in his shoulders, hear the unsteady catch of his breath. The sound hollowed her chest, and she hated that it did.

For a long moment neither spoke. The carriage swayed, the sound of the wheels beneath them a soft, rhythmic counterpoint to the tension hanging thick in the air.

"Bells," he murmured, lifting his head slightly. "I meant every word, but if you will not believe me, I understand and know I can do no more."

Her hands were cold, and she tucked them into her lap to keep from shaking, to keep from reaching for him. She wanted to scream, to cry, to strike him —but her voice betrayed her, small and tight.

He stayed where he was, looking up at her, until the carriage slowed. She refused to meet his eyes again, refused to let him see the tears that blurred her vision. "You should return home," she said quietly. "Have the driver upon returning you to Berkley Square to go back and wait for the duke and duchess."

When the footman opened the door, she rose and gathered her skirts. Whitmore slumped onto the opposite seat but did not say another word.

She stepped out, the air from outside cool against her heated cheeks, and climbed down without his help. Her legs trembled, her throat tight with everything said. She could still feel the ghost of his touch against her gown, the echo of his voice in her ears.

As the carriage door shut behind her, Isabella straightened her spine and walked toward her home. Her chest ached, but she would not falter.

If this was love, it was a cruel and treacherous thing—and she would never let it undo her again.

CHAPTER
TWENTY-SEVEN

The carriage jolted forward, but Hartley's body refused to move with it. He sat frozen, staring at the closed door where Isabella had just vanished. Every breath he took was a knife.

She was gone.

The faint scent of her perfume still clung to the seat across from him—roses and something heartbreakingly delicate. It made his chest ache in a way he could no longer bear.

"Damn this," he growled, shoving open the carriage door. "Damn this to hell."

The startled coachman barely managed to rein in the horses before Hartley leapt down into the street. "Return to the ball for the duke and duchess," he barked. "Do not wait for me."

He didn't wait for an answer, instead he strode toward the ducal townhouse, his boots striking the stone steps hard enough to echo through the quiet night. His pulse thundered in his ears. He could think of nothing but her—the way she'd looked at him, the ice in her voice, the tears she'd refused to shed. He could not lose her. Not like this.

Inside, the entryway was bright, the scent of wax polish heavy in the air. A startled footman nearly dropped the tray of glassware he carried.

"Where is Lady Isabella?"

"My—my lord, the lady—"

But Hartley was already moving. He saw her halfway up the grand staircase, her pale gown glinting softly in the light from the sconces above. "Bells!" he called.

She turned, eyes wide, shock flashing across her face. "What are you doing?" she hissed, glancing down into the hall. "You cannot be here—"

He took the stairs two at a time, closing the distance before she could protest further. He didn't think—he couldn't think. His heart was a storm, his only anchor her.

When he reached her, he caught her up in his arms.

She gasped, palms pressing against his chest. "Hartley! Put me down this instant. You cannot—"

"Where's your room?" he demanded, his voice low, rough, urgent.

"Don't you dare—"

"Where, Isabella?"

Her chin lifted, defiant. "At the end of the hall. But I swear, if you do not—"

He didn't let her finish.

Ignoring the servants' startled glances as he strode down the corridor with her in his arms, he muttered, "Let them talk. I care not what anyone thinks."

She squirmed against him, furious, her hands

pushing at his shoulders. "You're mad! You need to stop this—right now!"

"Not until you hear me," he said. "Not until you understand."

Her heartbeat thudded against his chest, a frantic rhythm that only drove him harder. The rustle of her skirts, the warmth of her breath near his throat, the way her body fit against his—all of it tangled his resolve into something wild and unbreakable.

He reached her room. Her maid, startled by their sudden entrance, froze mid-motion with a gown in her hands.

"My lord?"

"Leave us," he said sharply.

The maid hesitated only a second before fleeing, skirts rustling into the corridor. Hartley slammed the door, turned the key, and the soft snick of the lock felt final. He set Isabella down on the bed and stood back, wondering what he was going to do now.

She glared at him, cheeks flushed with fury. "You've lost your mind. If my sister finds out you're here—"

"I don't care," he said, stepping closer.

"The servants will tell—"

"Let them."

Her glare could have cut through glass. "You've no right to barge into my home like some—some barbarian!"

"Then call me one," he said quietly, "but I'm not leaving until you forgive me."

She gave a sharp, disbelieving laugh. "Forgive

you? You think one more intrusion will make me forget your wager? Your betrayal?"

He came closer still, the edge of the bed brushing his knees. "I think," he said, his voice low, "that I'll make you see that everything I said in that carriage was truth. That I love you, Isabella Ravensmere, and I will prove it."

She shook her head, but her voice faltered. "You can't force forgiveness."

"I don't intend to," he said. "I intend to earn it."

Her lips parted as though to retort, but he silenced her with a look—steady, unyielding, full of every ounce of feeling he'd denied for three long weeks. The longest in his life. Even his exile abroad seemed quicker than the time he'd spent away from her.

The air between them hummed. The lamplight caught the gold in her hair, the soft rise and fall of her chest. He could see the battle warring in her eyes—anger, pride, and something that looked dangerously close to longing.

"I will not leave this room," he said softly, "until you believe me. Until you know I mean every word I've said. By morning, you'll see that what I feel for you is not duty, not guilt, not scandal. It is love, pure and maddening, and I'll not let you go until you understand that."

Her breath trembled. "You're impossible."

He smiled faintly. "So you've told me before."

For a heartbeat, neither moved. Then, slowly, he reached out, his fingers brushing a stray curl from her cheek. She didn't pull away.

Her pulse fluttered beneath his fingertips. The faint hitch of her breath told him everything her words would not. "Bells," he whispered, "forgive me."

He leaned in, his mouth finding hers.

The world fell away.

Her lips were soft and unyielding, tasting faintly of defiance and something heartbreakingly sweet. Her hands came up to his chest—not to push him away this time, but to hold herself steady against the force of everything between them.

He deepened the kiss, and Hartley promised himself that no matter what waited beyond this night, he would never let her doubt his love again. He removed his jacket and waistcoat, kicked off his boots, and pulled his shirt from his breeches, before he rid himself of those too.

With relief, he watched as Isabella fought with the laces of her gown before he turned her about and all but ripped them from their ties, desperate to have her out of her dress. She stood, and the gown and stays fell to the floor before she slipped her shift over her head, leaving her in nothing but her silk stockings.

His breath caught at the delectable sight she made. She was so utterly perfect and beautiful—and his.

All his.

He cupped her face, kissing her, drinking from her mouth like a man starved of water. "I love you so much."

They tumbled onto the bed, and he kissed his way down her neck, marking her with his tongue and small love bites. He kneaded her breast, his mouth suckling one of her nipples, teasing the peaked, pink flesh. He could not get enough of her, he was mad with want and the demand to love her again.

She squirmed beneath him, her fingers spiking into his hair, fisting his locks, holding him as if she never wished to let go.

And he would not. She would never be rid of him.

He kissed his way down her smooth, flat stomach, reaching between her legs to slip his hand over her mons, teasing her wet, ready cunny. The proof of her desire was in equal measure relief and torture. She gasped and moaned when he slipped a finger into her, teasing her, readying her for what was to come.

Hartley could wait no longer. He moved lower and licked along her sweet, most private of places, teasing her with his tongue, suckling her until she was bucking beneath him. His name a plea, an appeal for more.

And he would give her more.

He worked her with his mouth, closing his eyes and relishing the taste of her. His cock was rock hard, his balls ached with denied release. He pressed himself into the bed, wanting a little relief from the torture he was enduring.

"Hartley..." His name on her lips almost undid him, and he suckled her harder, flicking his tongue over her engorged nubbin, wanting her to come. Wanting her to grind her quim on his face and take what he offered.

Thankfully he did not have to wait long. She tightened her legs about his face, a telltale sign she was near. He groaned, savoring the moment of her climax. He worked her sweet flesh until she was spent and sated, her legs lax and open, her body his to explore.

Only then did he kiss his way back to her mouth. He took her lips hard at the same time as he thrust into her with a determination—a declaration—that left them both breathless.

She wrapped her legs about his waist, and he rocked into her, kissing her, marking her his. "You're so beautiful. I will never get enough of you, my heart, my love, my everything."

She clasped his cheeks, watching him, her eyes glassy and hopeful.

"I would not be here now, I would not be fighting for you, Bells, if I did not want you to be mine. Please know—please believe me." He pushed hard, and she gasped, arching her back, her breasts rocking with the movement.

"Tell me you believe me. Tell me that you love me too, before I expire of wondering if it's only me who's affected by this emotion."

She met his eyes and they locked and held. "You are not alone in this new reality," she finally admitted.

"Thank God." He took her, thrusting into her until they were both without wits or breath. The first tremors of her release tightened about his cock, and he held on as long as he could before they came in a whirlwind of gasps and cries of delight, tumbling together over the edge of bliss.

After several heartbeats, he slumped to her side, pulling her close and knowing there would not be another night they would not lie like this. Married or not, he would never be separated from her again.

She slumped onto his chest, as if the weeks they

had been apart had never happened. He wished they had not—but he would make it up to her. "I will, from this day forward, strive to make you pleased. To never make you sad or disappointed with me again."

She glanced up at him, a small smile playing on her kiss-swollen lips. "We will argue about some things, Hartley. No marriage is perfect. But so long as you never enter another stupid wager like the one you did with the duke, we shall be well."

He slipped his hand into her hair, cupping the nape of her neck. "I will never be so foolish again, even if that thoughtlessness made me come to realize how much I love you. For that, I shall forever be grateful."

She made a little scoffing sound before wiggling into the crook of his arm. "You're lucky, I suppose, that the wager involved me. You could, right at this moment, find yourself betrothed to a woman you do not care for—and then where would you be? All because you were an irrational child who had to bet with his friend instead of saying no like an intelligent adult would."

Her words shamed him. It was only providence that such a situation had not occurred. "I see your point and agree. I promise I have learned my lesson."

"Good." She leaned up and cupped his face. "While I'm still a little mad at you, I do believe you—and I want what we started that first night together. I want a love match with you, Hartley. I love you too, so much. I was so hurt that you only courted me for a wager. It made me feel dirty and worth nothing more than a bit of amusement for two men I thought highly of. You hurt me."

His heart broke anew. "I know, and I'm so sorry. Truly. I promise to make it up to you."

An impish grin slipped onto her lips. "Well, what you did earlier was certainly interesting. I could like that again, I think—if you're willing, of course."

He moved his mouth near her ear, bussing it with a quick kiss before he whispered, "When my mouth was on your quim?"

A blush stole over her cheeks, and he chuckled.

"Yes, when your wicked tongue was between my legs."

Her bold words sent his cock to rigid in an instant. He rolled her onto her back, her legs spreading, willing and pliant for his every wish. "You do not know what you have started, my lady."

She ran her hand through his hair, her eyes shadowed with desire. "Oh, I think I do. I'm going to be marrying the worst rake in London. I think I know exactly what's to come next."

He grinned, kissing his way down her stomach.

Perhaps she did. Still, he had other tricks up his sleeve that she would soon enjoy. So much to look forward to.

Together.

EPILOGUE

The week had passed in a blur of fittings, flowers, and family. And now, standing in the grand ballroom of the ducal residence, Isabella could scarcely believe it was done—she was a married woman. Lady Isabella Ravensmere no more. The title still echoed through her mind like a bell she wasn't yet used to hearing.

The Marchioness of Whitmore.

She looked down at her wedding gown, the light-blue silk gleaming like a beautiful summer's day. Her sisters surrounded her, all smiles and laughter—Rosalind radiant as ever, Evangeline with tears in her eyes, Angelica and Cordelia ensuring everything went to their plan, and dear Clementine, newly arrived from the country and much improved after her health scare from the winter before. The sound of their chatter filled the room, a melody of love and teasing that warmed Isabella's heart.

"Do you think the cake is too extravagant?" Rosalind whispered, leaning close. "The baker swore the sugar roses would not droop, but they look perilously close to it."

"They're perfect," Isabella said, smiling. "Though I might never look at cake again without thinking of the trouble it caused."

Rosalind chuckled and gave her hand a squeeze. "You look beautiful, my darling. Mama would be so proud."

The words caught in Isabella's throat. She blinked back tears and looked across the ballroom to where Hartley stood with Ravensmere, both men laughing over some remark. The sunlight gilded his hair, catching the hint of gold at his temples. His gaze, when it found hers, softened in that way that made her heart turn over every single time.

It was still strange to think how close she had come to losing him—and how easily she might have hardened her heart against him forever. But love, she now understood, wasn't about perfection. It was about forgiveness, trust, and the courage to begin again.

When the violinists struck up another tune, she murmured her excuses to her sisters and crossed the floor toward him. The sight of her husband—her *husband*—standing there waiting for her made her stomach flutter like a debutante's.

"Are you enjoying your wedding breakfast, my lord?" she teased, taking his arm.

"Immensely," he replied, eyes glinting with mischief. "Though I confess, I'm rather tired of sharing you with our family. A moment's peace, Bells."

"I cannot imagine why," she said, smiling despite herself.

He bent his head close enough that only she could hear. “Because, my love, I married you to have you to myself.”

Her cheeks warmed, her pulse tripping at the intimacy in his tone. The scent of him—deliciously familiar—wrapped around her like a secret. A secret only she knew of.

He glanced toward their wedding cake that waited on the sideboard. “Come with me.”

“Hartley,” she whispered, laughing softly. “We cannot leave now.”

“Why not?”

“Because our family will notice.”

“Let them. I have a sudden and desperate craving for dessert...alone.”

Before she could protest further, he had procured a slice of the wedding cake and led her through a side door and into the quieter corridors of the house. Her heart raced, half-scandalized and wholly delighted as he tugged her along, their footsteps muffled by the thick Aubusson rugs.

They started up the stairs until he stopped before her old room. His grin was wicked. “Fitting, don’t you think?”

She rolled her eyes, but laughter bubbled from her lips. “You’re incorrigible.”

“Entirely.” He guided her inside and closed the door behind them.

The quiet of the room wrapped around them, broken only by the faint sound of the celebration below—the hum of music, the echo of distant laughter. It felt as though the world had narrowed to the two of them alone, suspended in a perfect moment.

"For the bride and groom," he said, lifting the plate of cake between them. "Shall we partake in a bite?"

"Of course."

They shared a bite each, laughter mingling with sweetness, crumbs on fingers and lips. Hartley set the plate down, moving to cup her face. "You have a little cake on your top lip." He did not move to remove it, instead he kissed her there, his tongue teasing her mouth with wicked intention.

She groaned, wanting him in an instant. "Tell me you did not bring me upstairs to seduce me."

He shrugged, walking backward until his knees hit one of the settees that sat before her fireplace. He slumped into the chair, watching her as his fingers nimbly ripped his falls open, exposing his rigid, sizeable cock.

Moisture pooled between her legs, and she straddled his lap without another word, desperate to have him. He shuffled her gown out of the way with a recklessness and desperation that left them without sense. Isabella took Hartley into her, wrapping her arms about his neck, riding him without shame, needing him to soothe the sweet ache between her thighs.

"God yes," he groaned, his hands a vise on her hips, working her upon him.

Isabella lost all sense. She took him, enjoyed the naughtiness of their situation, relished the feel only he evoked. Her body convulsed, trembled and tumbled into bliss far too quickly than she would have liked. Hartley's cry of pleasure mingled with hers and she kissed him, deep and long, knowing that she would never tire of him, would always want him this way.

That he was hers and she was his and nothing would ever change that fact.

"I adore you," he said, brushing his mouth against hers. "I will remember this day for the rest of my life, whether it be long or short, you are my everything."

Tears welled in her eyes, and she cupped his face. "I love you too."

When at last they returned downstairs, arm in arm, Rosalind's gaze found them immediately—suspicious, knowing—and Isabella bit the inside of her cheek to keep from laughing.

Hartley bent close. "Do you suppose they guessed where we went?" he whispered.

"Undoubtedly," she said, unable to keep the smile from her face. "Rosalind will never forgive us."

"Then we shall give her something else to talk about," he said, drawing her toward the dance floor.

She laughed softly as he led her into the impromptu waltz. Around them, their family stood, the air rich with music, the day full of celebration.

She lifted her gaze to his, her heart full. Whatever lay ahead, she knew one thing with certainty. They would face it together. And as he spun her beneath the glittering morning light basking the drawing room this day, Isabella smiled. For the first time in her life, it was her time to shine, and she was exactly where she was meant to be.

In Lord Hartley Whitmore's arms.

Who would have guessed...

DON'T MISS TAMARA'S OTHER ROMANCE SERIES

Heiress

Diamond of the Season

Treasure of the Ton

Jewel of the Ball

Ruby in the Rough

Gilded in Sin

1777 Society

One Night in London

Midnight in Mayfair

An Evening to Remember

Dalliance and Dukes

My Virtuous Duke

My Notorious Rogue

My Ruthless Beau

The Wayward Yorks

A Wager with a Duke

My Reformed Rogue

Wild, Wild, Duke

In the Duke of Time

Duke Around and Find Out

The Wayward Woodvilles

A Duke of a Time

On a Wild Duke Chase

Speak of the Duke

Every Duke has a Silver Lining

One Day my Duke Will Come

Surrender to the Duke

My Reckless Earl

Brazen Rogue

The Notorious Lord Sin

Wicked in My Bed

League of Unweddable Gentlemen

Tempt Me, Your Grace

Hellion at Heart

Dare to be Scandalous

To Be Wicked With You

Kiss Me, Duke

The Marquess is Mine

Kiss the Wallflower

A Midsummer Kiss

A Kiss at Mistletoe

A Kiss in Spring

To Fall For a Kiss

A Duke's Wild Kiss

To Kiss a Highland Rose

To Marry a Rogue

Only an Earl Will Do

Only a Duke Will Do

Only a Viscount Will Do

Only a Marquess Will Do

Only a Lady Will Do

Lords of London

To Bedevil a Duke

To Madden a Marquess

To Tempt an Earl

To Vex a Viscount

To Dare a Duchess

To Marry a Marchioness

Royal House of Atharia

To Dream of You

A Royal Proposition

Forever My Princess

A Time Traveler's Highland Love

To Conquer a Scot

To Save a Savage Scot

To Win a Highland Scot

A Stolen Season

A Stolen Season

A Stolen Season: Bath

A Stolen Season: London

Scandalous London

A Gentleman's Promise

A Captain's Order

A Marriage Made in Mayfair

High Seas & High Stakes

His Lady Smuggler

Her Gentleman Pirate

A Wallflower's Christmas Wreath

Daughters Of The Gods

Banished

Guardian

Fallen

Stand Alone Books

Defiant Surrender

A Brazen Agreement

To Sin with Scandal

Outlaws

ABOUT THE AUTHOR

Tamara is an Australian author who grew up in an old mining town in country South Australia, where her love of history was founded. So much so, she made her darling husband travel to the UK for their honeymoon, where she dragged him from one historical monument and castle to another.

A mother of three, her two little gentlemen in the making, a future lady (she hopes) keep her busy in the real world, but whenever she gets a moment's peace she loves to write romance novels in an array of genres, including regency, medieval and time travel.